"I UNDERST… FOLEY THA… …CALL YOURSELF A PRIVATE INVESTIGATOR?"

"All Confidential Missions and Enquiries cheerfully and promptly undertaken," Hooky assured him. "Any law against it?"

"There ought to be," Fred Dale said sharply.

"Live and let live, Inspector."

"Live and let live has nothing to do with it. Catching criminals is a police job. When it comes to villainy, crime, leave it to us, Mr. Hefferman. That's what we are paid for; not enough, but that's another matter."

"So you don't want any help?" Hooky asked, beginning to feel a little annoyed.

"Don't start trying to do things on your own. We'll take all the necessary action. Got it?"

"You're a very forthright man, Inspector."

————————— ★ —————————

THE
FAIRLY
INNOCENT
LITTLE MAN

LAURENCE
MEYNELL

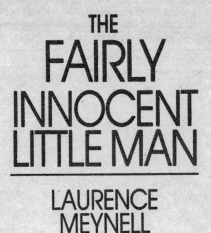

W❂RLDWIDE.

TORONTO • NEW YORK • LONDON
AMSTERDAM • PARIS • SYDNEY • HAMBURG
STOCKHOLM • ATHENS • TOKYO • MILAN
MADRID • WARSAW • BUDAPEST • AUCKLAND

THE FAIRLY INNOCENT LITTLE MAN

A Worldwide Mystery/August 1992

This edition is reprinted by arrangement with
Scarborough House.

ISBN 0-373-26102-0

for Rachel,
my hostess at Aldenham Park

ONE

AN EAST WIND blew along the Lawns, a watery sun was making a poor business of setting behind Shoreham and out at sea the skies were wet and grey.

Hooky couldn't raise much enthusiasm for the *mise-en-scène* and was already regretting that he had come.

Regret was however tinged with the philosophic reflection that in effect he had had but little choice in the matter. Invitations from his Aunt were rarities and when they arrived they had the force and inescapability of Royal Commands.

'Dear Nephew' (the letter had run)

'I want you to stay here for the week-end after next. No doubt this will mean your giving up some expensive race meeting, or one of those disreputable parties you are constantly attending, but that cannot be helped. I am having a Bridge evening here in my flat on the Friday and I want you to make up my four. I have taken up Bridge lately and find that I am quite good at it. Do not arrive before six, please and not a minute later than half past. We'll start to play at seven. If you have let your Bridge get rusty kindly brush it up before Friday.

Your affectionate Aunt,
Theresa Page-Foley.'

This forthright communication had been slapped down on Hooky's table with the other and less impressive items of mail by Roly Watkins, the factotum of the dilapidated house in Gerrard Mews, Soho, where Hooky lived and conducted a permanently ailing business as a private investigator.

Like all his Aunt's letters it was intriguing. As far as he knew Bridge was a new venture for the formidable old woman, and Hooky could well imagine that she would be pretty terrifying at it.

A life with some rough passages in it up and down the world, playing the role of gentleman adventurer with zest and generally cocking a snook at fate, had left Hooky Hefferman unafraid of most things. He had been case-hardened so that he didn't scare easily; but he had a very healthy respect for his Aunt, the Honourable Theresa Page-Foley. It was impossible to imagine anybody, even Life itself, taking liberties with her.

On one memorable occasion she had paid a state visit to Gerrard Mews to see for herself where her nephew lived and worked. It had taken Roly Watkins several days to recover from the shock of the visitation and he still frequently referred to it.

'My God, that Honourable Aunt of yours, Mr Hefferman,' he said, 'if she was to appear on *What's*

Your Line they'd guess it at once. No trouble at all. Lion tamer in chief to Billy Smart's Circus.'

Yet Hooky couldn't help feeling a curious and admiring affection for the brave old lady. An anachronistic relic from a vanished world of green baize doors, ladies' maids, butlers and liveried chauffeurs, she uncompromisingly faced the sad new times in which she found herself; asking no quarter and certainly giving none. There was also the consideration that the Hon. Mrs P-F possessed a great deal of money. You might not think so from some of the petty economies that she enjoyed making but she was in fact a very rich woman. She had once told Hooky, 'When I die I shall leave some money to you Hooky. It is very unlikely to do you good. I realise that, of course. But if you are going to the devil anyway you may as well go in comfort. I did think of leaving everything to the South Sussex Home for Distressed Cats but I found the secretary so intolerably bourgeois. The people you mix with are villains and reprehensible characters but at least they aren't bourgeois.'

Hooky was one of those remarkable people who never seem to have any money and who yet manage to live extremely well. Few people enjoyed spending money more than he did, but he couldn't be bothered to regard getting it as a main purpose of life, so the fact that his Aunt might one day leave him a fortune was not the chief reason for paying her a visit occasionally. Hooky went to Hove every now and again because the formidable old lady fascinated and terrified him. Visiting that unyielding chunk of Victorian individualism was an emotional experience, and Hooky was an amateur of experiences.

Traffic on the A23 had been unexpectedly light so that he had made good time and had arrived well before six. Even people who knew Mrs Page-Foley only slightly soon realised that it was safest to take most of what she said literally, particularly in regard to time. If Mrs Page-Foley decided that she wanted you to dine with her the matter was not concluded over the telephone, casually and inexactly in the modern manner... *oh, round about eight I suppose... that sort of time... eightish if that suits you...* nothing of that sort for Mrs Page-Foley; an invitation from her came through the post, formally, even imperiously worded. At the bottom of the card would be added in her thin spidery aristocratic handwriting 'Dinner will be at eight, please come at ten minutes before that time'; and the printed injunction R.S.V.P. would be twice underlined to remind you that you belonged to a generation whose manners were not to be trusted.

Hooky, of course, was well aware of his Aunt's peculiarity in this matter; it was, in fact, one of the traits which endeared her to him, so that finding himself in Hove when his dashboard clock still said no more than a quarter to six he naturally did not make the elementary mistake of going straight to her flat. '*Do not arrive before six and not a minute later than half past*...the instructions had been refreshingly clear and uncomplicated. Hooky sometimes found himself wishing that politicians, parsons and the whole tribe of muddled thinking experts who discussed every subject under the sun on the box or the radio in hesitant, repetitive, ungrammatical half sentences would take English lessons from his Aunt.

Finding himself with twenty minutes or more to spare he parked his ancient and beloved Jag and went to stretch his legs on the Lawns.

The east wind, and the rain which was already beginning to fall in heavy spots with the ominous threat of more to come, were not encouraging and the sight of a fat over-fed woman leading a fat over-fed dog and waiting patiently whilst it lifted its leg against a Corporation notice saying 'Do not let your Dog Foul these Lawns' soon lost its attraction. Hooky decided to give them best and to seek refuge in The Raven.

The Raven was hidden away in what, in more spacious days, had been a Mews. It was not a particularly good pub, but at least it *was* a pub; and it had the great advantage of being close to Mrs Page-Foley's flat. Hooky was a pub man; he was at his best in pubs; he understood pubs. Like every aficionado he knew that every pub had its individuality, its *persona*, its set of unwritten rules and customs which the true addict recognises by instinct and is anxious to obey. The Raven had never come high on Hooky's list; but it was better than the east wind and the lawn-fouling fat dog.

Only one other customer was there, talking loudly to a bored looking barmaid. Hooky had never seen the man before, yet in a sense he knew him only too well. The cavalry twill trousers encasing legs that had never been astride a horse; the tweed jacket with leather shoulder insets on which a gun had never been carried; the fly tucked into the band of a hat which had never seen a salmon; the almost brand new, uncreased, suede shoes; the over-loud voice puffing out the condescending syllables '...*of course you wouldn't remember, my dear, before your time, what?...*' all these things were so much in character that they were almost stage props.

'*Floreat Hovea*' thought Hooky as he ordered his double Teachers with a minimum of water, a necessary precaution against the alcoholic stringency of his Aunt's flat, where one small, insufficiently dry, sherry was apt to be considered adequate alcoholic cushioning against the rigours and pressures of existence.

'...*the riff-raff from Brighton,*' the synthetic gentleman at the bar was now saying to the barmaid. It was evidently the concluding passage of a Declaration of Self-righteous Condemnation which the long suffering woman had listened to many times before. She nodded abstractedly, polishing a glass as she did so.

Tweed coat and twill trousers drained the last of his pink gin, puffed out his lips in a curious little explosive sound, and departed.

Hooky caught the barmaid's eye. She hadn't seen him before; not one of her regulars; but there was something about him, his eye, his chunkiness, his 'to-hell-with-the-lot-of-them' air which she liked.

A moment previously she had been bored to tears; now she smiled a little. Hooky (God help him!) had always had that effect on women. They might like him or violently dislike him, but they were disturbed by him; they wanted to know more about him. 'Friend of yours?' Hooky said, nodding in the direction of the door.

'You get all sorts,' she answered cryptically. Hooky laughed at the words. Good pub philosophy; you did, indeed, get all sorts; it was a definition of the great round glorious world; infinitely infuriating, unendingly interesting. He pushed his glass forward. 'Double Teachers please.'

'I just this moment gave you one.'

'There was a hole in the glass.'

She dealt with the matter of the disappearing Teachers and leaning over her bar confided to Hooky, 'I can't stand men with deaf-aids; he's got a deaf-aid, did you notice? And a glass eye, too. It sort of upsets me!' Hooky wanted to say, 'Give the poor gink two plastic balls and a tin tool and he'll be fully qualified to walk up and down the front as an independent English gentleman sound in wind and limb,' but he didn't want to offend the barmaid; she might, after all, not be a devotee of the Royal Court Theatre.

He glanced at the clock. It said 6.15.

'Pub time?' he enquired.

'No, actually it's right.'

Hooky dealt with the Teachers and said, 'Then I must be moving. Fate calls!'

'I wish it would call me.'

'I have to go and meet my Aunt.'

'Some Aunt,' said the barmaid in amused disbelief as she watched him go out into the street.

Mrs Page-Foley lived in the extremely expensive ground floor flat of one of the most modern and hideous buildings in the town. Time had been when she was the mistress of an establishment in the country with three acres of garden complete with huge herbaceous border and espaliered peach trees on the sun-drenched south wall. 'Thank goodness all that's finished with,' she would sometimes say, 'Digby and I didn't own the place, the gardeners did. McCulloch, our head mean, had been at Chatsworth and had never got over it. I daren't do a thing without getting his permission first. Now I haven't even a pot-plant to look after and I'm very glad of it.' In the herbaceous border and pluck-your-own-peaches-for-breakfast days entering the house had been a matter of liveried footmen and stately butler formality; in Hove that, too, had changed.

Arriving at Wensdale Court Hooky found himself confronted by a board with a number of bell-pushes and a slatted metal arrangement beneath them. 'Ring and speak,' advised a laconic instruction. He rang the bell of the ground floor flat and in a few seconds a familiar voice, unfairly distorted by the mechanisms of the device, barked at him through the metal louvres.

'Who is that?'

'Hooky here, Aunt T.'

'I'll open the door and when you are in be quite sure that you shut it behind you please.'

Mrs Page-Foley then pressed a switch in the living-room of her flat and Hooky heard the complicated lock of the front door click as it was released by remote control.

He made his way in and shut the door carefully behind him. The front door of his Aunt's flat stood some ten paces away across the circular foyer and it was ajar. Hooky approached it with a slight twinge of the visiting-the-headmaster's-study feeling which always assailed him when about to see the formidable old lady inside.

The formidable old lady looked, as she always did, in good parade order. She might live alone, she might despise the world in which she now found herself stranded; but inflexible standards remained. She was never other than well dressed, never other than in full command of herself and the situation. Indeed, on this occasion, it struck Hooky that she looked even better than usual.

'How smart you look Aunt T,' he said.

She affected to be scornful; but no woman who has been to her hairdresser that afternoon and taken trouble choosing the black dress and the pearls to go with it really minds being told that the result has been noticed.

'Smart indeed!' she replied. 'Don't be ridiculous. Have you just arrived?'

'More or less.'

'I suppose that means you have been wasting the last half hour or so in one of those low public houses you are so fond of frequenting.'

'What a suspicious mind you've got!' Hooky protested, laughing.

'I'm a woman,' his Aunt reminded him, 'and women have to have suspicious minds. Self-defence. Nature arranges things that way. Like camouflage. Well, if you haven't been drinking already you can start now. The Waterford decanter is full of whisky. Teachers I believe it is called. Major Weller seems to prefer that brand.'

'Sensible fellow,' Hooky said, hastening to take advantage of this welcome change in the custom of the establishment, and at the same time speculating with considerable interest as to who Major Weller might be. Was it possible, he wondered, that the smart black dress, the string of pearls and the general air of being dressed for an occasion, was it possible, he wondered, that these were indications of anything sensational? His studied his Aunt covertly. She was old and in a long life she had known a lot of changes; she had seen the old established order burn up and wither away. Yet she was a woman; and with women, as Hooky was only too well aware, you could never tell... He looked forward with interest to meeting Major Weller...

'Our fourth,' Mrs Page-Foley went on in her sharp staccato way, 'is Laetitia Bitterne. Lady Bitterne. Very aptly named, too. *Boom, boom, boom*. How she hates losing. Almost as much as I dislike her winning. Unless you propose to sit there drinking whisky indefinitely perhaps you would help in arranging the room.'

Hooky leapt to his feet and busied himself setting out the card table and chairs under his Aunt's direction.

It was not altogether a simple matter for Theresa Page-Foley had an acquisitive nature and when she had been forced to abandon her once grand style of living and from an eighteen room country house had contracted (thankfully, as she always insisted) into a three room flat she had brought the majority of her possessions with her. The result was that her living-room at Hove was crammed to overflowing. There was a lot of good furniture in it, an astonishing amount of bric-a-brac, a positive gallery of signed photographic portraits and of course the collection of snuff-boxes. There were forty-two of them, every one a collector's piece and the whole lot worth some fabulous sum which Hooky never even bothered to think about. He didn't take snuff and wasn't interested in snuff-boxes, but the huge flat glass topped case containing the things was a nuisance when you were trying, as he was now, to get a card table in position and to manoeuvre four chairs and the necessary little side tables round it.

Whilst he was busy doing this his Aunt questioned him sharply about the state of his Bridge. 'I hope you've been playing regularly,' she said. 'Although, of course, the trouble with you, Hooky, is that you never do anything regularly, do you—except drink, I suppose. You never stick to anything. Hover-hover; flibberty-gibbet; no stamina. Typically modern.'

'I suppose you were modern once,' Hooky ventured to say.

'If I ever was I've forgotten it, it was so long ago,' his Aunt answered testily. 'Don't think it's any fun at all being old; because it isn't.'

Hooky believed her.

'And what about your Bridge?'

'Not to worry,' he reassured her. 'I expect I'll get by.'

A number of things had come easily to Hooky Hefferman for almost as long as he could remember—making love to a pretty woman, drinking good malt whisky and playing any form of card game being high on the list. He had played Poker all over the world, often enough for desperate stakes in dangerous company; he had sat down to Bridge with venom-tongued matrons at Crockford's and found that sec-

ond experience considerably the more frightening of
the two. Although not in completely full practice he
flattered himself that he could hold his own in his
Aunt's domestic four in Wensdale Court.

Asking Theresa Page-Foley questions about herself
was always a chancy business, as he knew from experience. You might be lucky enough to tap a well of
fascinating autobiography, or you might get your head
bitten off for your impertinent curiosity. Nevertheless
Hooky was intrigued to hear what had given his Aunt
her recently discovered interest in Bridge, and she
seemed willing enough, almost anxious indeed, to tell
him.

' . . . I used to play a lot with Digby in the old days.
He was passionately fond of a game. Of course that
was long before Contract came in and as for things like
Acol and all the rest of it, why the words didn't even
exist. Then I let it drop for years; until a couple of
months ago in fact, when I ran across Laetitia Bitterne at a party. Laetitia and I hadn't seen one another for—oh, I'm not going to tell you how long.
She's older than I am, though she won't admit it, of
course, but she is, by a full year. I had no idea she was
going to be at this party I went to. I don't suppose I
had given her a thought in twenty years. Then *boom,
boom, boom*, I heard coming across the room, and I
thought *good gracious that must be Laetitia Bitterne*.
She never was a good-looking woman; Digby used to
say if you clapped a saddle on her and sent her down

to the starting post for the four-thirty nobody would know the difference. But she was somebody out of the old world, somebody who knew the things and people I used to know, so of course we got talking again.

'"But what do you *do* with yourself all the time?" she asked.

'I told her that one way and another there was plenty to do.

'"But there just *isn't*," she insisted, "Heavens, if I didn't have the Club to go to I think I should go mad."

'As a matter of fact I always regarded Laetitia as being slightly mad, but I didn't think it the moment to say so; instead I asked her what club she was talking about.

'"The Fothergill. A Bridge Club. I play there practically every afternoon. Last week I won over three pounds. Why don't you come along—if you think you could still play."

'I wasn't having Laetitia Bitterne saying that sort of thing to me; as long as we had known one another I could always do anything she could do, and generally rather better. And although I had told her that I always had plenty to do it wasn't strictly true. She's the sort of person it isn't wise to tell the whole truth to. Quite often in the afternoon here I *don't* have anything to do and occasionally I have found time hanging a big heavily. So I got her to introduce me to the Fothergill and I became a member. The Club runs a special beginners' session every afternoon and I soon found I was getting the hang of things again. And of course I don't like being called a *beginner* at anything. If I'm going to do a thing at all I like to do it properly. And I certainly wasn't going to have Laetitia Bitterne crowing—*booming*—over me. I asked the woman who runs the Club, Mrs Medhurst, what to do and she said why not get Major Weller to give you some lessons.'

'And who is Major Weller?' Hooky enquired, injudiciously as it turned out.

'The trouble with you, Hooky, is that you never listen. You're too much of an extrovert. You're so busy giving out all the time that you don't have time to take anything in. I have already explained to you that Major Weller is our fourth this evening.'

'And he drinks Teachers? Right?'

'Unlike you, Hooky, Major Weller is usually content with one small whisky and soda in the course of the evening. He is an extremely pleasant, well-mannered man, very fond of Bridge, who has kindly agreed to visit me for tea three or four times and help me to bring my somewhat rusty play up to date. And by the way, before they come let me make quite clear what the stakes are: I never play for more than one and a half pence a hundred.'

Hooky smiled submissively and amiably. He had long since learnt it is never much use doing anything else when the old autocrat of Wensdale Court issued her *fiats*.

'Put plenty of ash trays about,' she ordered. 'You smoke continually, of course, and so does Laetitia Bitterne. It's a disgusting habit, but it reduces the population, you smokers kill yourselves off quite easily thank goodness, and it helps to pay the national debt so I suppose one shouldn't do anything to discourage it.'

The bell rang and Mrs Page-Foley spoke down the inter-com.

'Yes, who is it?'

A voice strongly reminiscent of a heavily laden coaster feeling her way up to the Port of London on a foggy November afternoon came through the speaking tube.

'Laetitia Bitterne here and I've got Major Weller with me.' Hooky's Aunt pressed the device which released the catch of the front door and said, 'You see what I mean about boom, boom, boom.'

When the visitors came into the flat Hooky being a keen student of the human kind looked at them both with interest. *There's nowt so queer as folk* was a dictum in which he firmly believed and which he had seen confirmed a hundred times in every part of the world. The teeming sea of humanity certainly had some odd fish in it; but the two thrown up on the shore of his Aunt's flat that evening were, he had to confess, disappointing specimens. Hooky felt certain that on any afternoon throughout the year he could have gone into a dozen Bridge clubs in Hove and found them stuffed with Laetitia Bitternes. The heavy-hands over-jewelled with rings; the jowls too fleshy through self-indulgent eating; the sharp eyes piercing percep-tive; the voice aggressive; the mathematics merci-lessly correct when it came to totting up winnings; interest in any conversation beyond the immediate re-quirement of the table *nil*.

Hooky, of course, had never met the late Sir Ben-jamin Bitterne, but he congratulated the old boy heartily on having had the sense to pack it in.

The other member of the four, Major Weller, had nothing disagreeable about him at all, he was a mild, inoffensive little man, as dapper and neat in his un-assuming appearance as he was precise in his speech. The more Hooky considered the little man the less was it possible to imagine any sort of romantic develop-ment between him and Aunt Theresa. To picture his Aunt in the matrimonial bed with anybody was a pretty awe-inspiring thought and it was clear that lit-tle Major Weller would not have survived two rounds of the contest, so Hooky had regretfully to abandon the tentative ideas which had been beginning to as-semble in his mind of seeing some form of autumnal flowering of the spirit in Wensdale Court. He gave that thought up at once and, helped by his Aunt's prompting, concentrated on Bridge.

'Hooky, don't stand there mooning. We want to start playing. That's what we are here for, you know. Cut.'

Hooky obediently cut.

He drew the Ace of Spades and Lady Bitterne the Ace of Hearts.

'You and I,' she boomed at him. 'Take the red cards.'

'No. I think I'll have the blue.'

'Blue, an unlucky colour.'

'Not for me,' Hooky said smiling sweetly at her, 'I'm sure we shall do well together.'

When the recording Angel finally casts up the account of Hooky Hefferman deceased certain entries will undoubtedly have to be made in the debit side, such as enthusiastic lechery, rather more than occasional drunkenness and a general sort of cussed disposition to poke his nose (twice broken) into other people's affairs to find out what was going on just for the hell of it; against these debit entries certainly one credit will have to be recorded—Hooky had a natural ability for card playing. He had a feeling for the thing and he was blessed with something invaluable for Bridge—a photographic memory. After a round of bidding and two rounds of play Hooky was usually able to make a ninety per cent correct estimate of all the cards his two opponents had in their hands. But really to enjoy any indoor sport, as Hooky was well aware, it is necessary to feel *simpatico* with one's partner; and with his partner in the first rubber of the evening Hooky found it quite impossible even to begin to feel *simpatico*.

After every hand a searching post-mortem was carried out at the full power of her fog-horn voice and any shortcomings, real or imaginary, in Hooky's calling or play were mercilessly dissected. Hooky realised that in the circumstances all he could do was to put up with it. Satisfying as it would have been to tell this horse-faced terror of the Fothergill Club exactly where she got off he had to admit that the shot wasn't on the board. Boom—boom had to be endured for the sake of Aunt Theresa and in the interest of general peace and quiet—two conditions which in spite of a number of tempestuous episodes in his life Hooky valued highly.

The built-in unpleasantness of Laetitia Bitterne was largely offset by the agreeable amiability of little Major Weller. Mrs Page-Foley—his partner in the first rubber—played what the most charitable commentator would have had to call an erratic game. Her wildest extravagances of calling or play never drew more than a smile and a gently tendered word of advice from Major Weller. At the finish of the first rubber Laetitia Bitterne announced triumphantly, 'I make that eighteen hundred. Let me see, you insist on playing for one and half p. don't you Theresa? So you owe me twenty-seven p. in this ridiculous new money.'

'It isn't ridiculous at all,' Mrs Page-Foley replied tartly. 'Digby always said that the decimal system was the only sane one to adopt. And I really don't know why you have to fall in with this terrible modern cus-

tom of talking about so many *p*, Laetitia. Perhaps you
don't understand that every pound is divided into one
hundred pence, and what I owe you now therefore is
correctly described as twenty-seven pence; not twenty-
seven *p*.'

Laetitia Bitterne extended a claw-like hand. 'Well,
pay it,' she said.

In the second rubber the two men played together
and as luck would have it held hardly a card between
them. 'Sorry partner,' Hooky had to say more than
once, 'I just haven't got a thing for you.'

The little Major remained unruffled. 'Fortune is
favouring the fair,' he said with a smile, 'and one can't
really grumble about that.'

To describe either his Aunt Theresa or Laetitia Bitterne as 'the fair' seemed to Hooky to be almost an
heroic exercise in politeness; but all his life he had
liked a good loser and he admired his partner's good-
natured acceptance of a run of atrocious luck. Totting up at the end of the second rubber Laetitia Bitterne said, 'You see, Theresa, when you play with me
you win.'

'Only because we held all the cards. I didn't understand a word of your calling.'

'Perhaps it's too advanced for you, dear.'

'I abominate things which call themselves *advanced*,' Mrs Page-Foley said.

Major Weller caught Hooky's eye, and he extended his glass saying mildly, 'I wonder if I might have another whisky and soda. Very weak, please.'

'Of course.'

Hooky jumped up full of gratitude and indeed of admiration for the little man's tact and bravery in intervening between the two mastodons.

It thus came about that for the final rubber of the evening Hooky found himself as partner to his Aunt. By this time he had had a chance to observe her peculiar style of play and was at least to some extent prepared for vagaries and sudden flights of fancy in her calling which would otherwise have left him bewildered.

Fortune, which in the middle of the evening had dealt so scurvily with him, now decided to smile broadly and she positively poured aces, kings and queens and highly convenient voids into the hands he picked up. Meanwhile Major Weller was enduring with the greatest good humour the totally unjustified criticisms and complaints which his partner levelled at him at the end of every hand.

'Too good to last,' Hooky told himself and he was suddenly proved right for he came most abruptly from riches to rags and dealt himself a hand containing only one card higher than a nine—the King of Spades. It was clear from the calling that his Aunt held nothing either, and Laetitia Bitterne, hardly troubling to con-

ceal her growing satisfaction proceeded happily to bid
a small slam in hearts.

'This will do something to retrieve things,' she said,
and when Major Weller put his hand down as dummy
she, for once, saw nothing to criticise in his bidding.

Mrs Page-Foley had to lead and Hooky waited with
interest to see what card fate and inspiration would
persuade her to produce. After a good deal of hesita-
tion she produced the Ace of Diamonds and said, 'I
really don't know whether it's the right card to play or
not; I've been trying to remember what you told me,
Major Weller, about leading against a slam call.'

'You shouldn't discuss matters in the middle of
play,' Laetitia Bitterne boomed. 'Is isn't ethical.'

'Don't be silly, Laetitia,' Mrs Page-Foley riposted
tartly. 'In my own drawing-room, over my own Bridge
table, I shall discuss what I like. And what do you
mean—*ethical?* It's a ridiculous word. I'm not at all
sure that you know the meaning of it. Getting a lot of
good cards in your hand all at once has gone to your
head.'

The Ace of Diamonds was a very welcome sight for
Hooky; he had hardly hoped to find such treasure in
his Aunt's hand. To attain the slam the remaining
twelve tricks had now to be won and it was clear right
from the start—and increasingly so after three rounds
had been played and trumps drawn—that this depended on the spade finesse. The calling made it obvious that Laetitia Bitterne held the Ace and Queen of

Spades; she would therefore, surely, lead a small spade from dummy; in pious hope more than any real expectation of good Hooky would also play small; Laetitia Bitterne would then play her Queen, the finesse would have succeeded and the contract be secure.

Since this was so obviously the correct line of play Hooky never suspected that things would take any other course. Yet, in a way, they did.

A small spade was indeed led from dummy and Hooky holding the King, nine and seven, played the nine. Laetitia Bitterne then hesitated. She was suddenly beset by doubt. Should she take the finesse or not? If the King was on the wrong side and the finesse failed the defence would make two diamond tricks; if she scorned the finesse and put up the Ace there was a distinct possibility that Theresa Page-Foley held a singleton King and there would be the delightful sight of it falling ignominiously to its ruin thus leaving the slam certain. Greed and a hatred of being beaten made Laetitia Bitterne lose her nerve. Finding herself suddenly in doubt she did what she not infrequently did at the Bridge table. She cheated. Mrs Page-Foley was holding her cards somewhat carelessly and Laetitia Bitterne shot a quick sideways glance at them.

Hooky happened to be watching her at that moment and saw her do it. He had not the slightest shadow of a doubt about what he had seen. '...*the old devil,*' he thought; if luck went against him in any game and he lost Hooky could grin and bear it as

cheerfully as the next man; but he had a very strong
objection to being conned.

Laetitia Bitterne's dishonourable sideways glance
was completed in less than a second. But it sufficed.
It told her what she wanted to know. The King of
Spades was not on the dangerous side of her and she
could safely take the finesse. She took it triumphantly and knew there was now only the formality of
playing out the five remaining cards and claiming the
slam.

When three of those cards had been played Hooky
suddenly spoke up in well simulated surprise. 'Hallo,
you've got two cards left haven't you?' 'Of course I
have,' Laetitia Bitterne said sharply, 'There are two
tricks still to be played. We've all got two cards, left.'

'I haven't,' Hooky told her, smiling blandly, 'Only
one.'

'But you *must* have two.'

Hooky spread his hands in apparent dismay. 'I'm
frightfully sorry,' he said, 'but no. There's no *must*
about it. I just *haven't* got two cards, that's all there
is to it.'

'Look on the floor, you must have dropped it.'

Everybody searched everywhere: under the table,
under their chairs, in the crevices of the seat Hooky
was sitting in; but without success.

'We must have been a card short at the beginning of
the deal,' Hooky said.

'Nobody said anything about a mis-deal,' Laetitia Bitterne pointed out.

'None of us noticed it obviously.'

'But I had a certain slam, all the rest of the tricks were mine.'

Anyone would have thought from the tone of Hooky's voice that he really was commiserating with her when he answered, 'Bad luck Lady Bitterne. I'm afraid we've got to look on it as a mis-deal and call the hand void.'

'I shall look it up in the rules tomorrow at the Club,' she told him, 'and if I find you are wrong I shall certainly send you the bill for the amount you owe me.'

'You do that,' Hooky agreed equably.

The evening therefore ended on a distinctly chilly note and when her guests had gone Mrs Page-Foley said, 'That beastly old *boom-boom-er*. What a fuss she made. What *can* have happened to that card Hooky?'

Hooky put his hand into a side pocket and drew out the three of clubs.

'Good heavens, you've found it?'

'I put it there. When Lady Bitterne was trying to make up her mind whether to take the finesse in spades or not she settled the matter by taking a damned good look at your hand, Aunt.'

'I never held anything except the Ace of Diamonds.'

'That's not the point. The point is that the Bitterne creature quite openly and deliberately cheated. I saw her do it, and I didn't see why she should get away with it.'

'Well, I'm obliged to you Hooky for taking action in the matter, and I certainly never object to taking Laetitia Bitterne down a peg or two; but really you took the whole thing too seriously. Just like a man to make a fuss over the inessential things. A little bit of cheating at cards? What of it? I always cheat if it's necessary and if I think I can get away with it!'

Hooky stared at his Aunt in astonishment. 'No comment,' he said at last. 'Women are extraordinary beings.'

Theresa Page-Foley nodded brightly. 'On the whole it was a very pleasant evening,' she said. 'We might have the same four again next week-end?' Hooky shook his head. He had had enough of that for the time being.

'I'm afraid I shall be busy next week-end,' he answered.

'Party after party,' his Aunt said reprovingly, 'what a dissolute life you do lead, Hooky.'

TWO

THE MAN calling himself Major Weller walked from Mrs Page-Foley's expensive flat along the sea front back towards the private hotel where he was staying. A neatly dressed, well-turned out little man enjoying a breath of sea-air after the evening's Bridge.

He smiled when he thought about the Bridge, particularly when he thought about the slam hand in which one card had so mysteriously disappeared. He thought it quite possible that the chunky-faced fellow, who had turned out to be the old girl's nephew, had lost it deliberately; he looked as though he was capable of that sort of thing, in fact he looked capable of quite a lot of things; he was a new portent on the horizon and one that would have to be watched.

Weller noticed that in one or two of the shelters along the front some of the glass panels had been smashed, clearly by deliberate vandalism. The sight distressed and annoyed him, he liked to live life in as orderly, well-behaved and comfortable a manner as possible. He turned in from the front and made his way into the quiet little square in which his private hotel stood. The Colwyn suited him admirably; it was reasonable in its terms, it was clean (and he had a passion for cleanliness) and the cooking had a pleasant homely flavour about it. When he went in Mrs Bell, the proprietress, who seemed to be on hand, and always cheerfully so, for about eighteen hours out of every twenty-four, was in the tiny cubby hole off the front hall which served as an office.

She emerged to welcome her favourite resident.

'A letter for you, Major Weller,' she said.

'Ah, good. Thank you.' Weller took the proffered envelope with apparent satisfaction and put it in his pocket.

'A mild evening, Major,' Mrs Bell said.

'Very. I walked back along the front and it was delightful.'

'I hope you enjoyed your Bridge?'

Major Weller smiled. 'Oh I always do. You must let me teach you sometime, Mrs Bell.'

'Oh go on with you, Major Weller! You know quite well that I haven't the time; and I'm not clever enough anyway.'

'I'm quite sure you are clever enough to do anything you want to,' Weller said, and he went upstairs to his room leaving behind a woman purring with pleasure.

Weller's room was small but comfortable. It was excessively tidy. And his suits hung neatly from coathangers; three pairs of well-polished shoes were lined up against one wall; on the dressing-table hair brushes, clothes brush and various toilet bottles stood in symmetrical array. Mrs Bell found it all highly satisfactory; 'Just what you would expect from a military gentleman,' she told her friends, happily ignorant of the fact that 'Major Weller's' title was one which the War Office knew nothing about; he had bestowed it on himself.

Weller's first act on gaining the privacy of his room was to draw the envelope from his pocket and, without bothering to open it, to tear it up and put the pieces neatly into the waste-paper basket. He didn't trouble to look inside the envelope because he knew there was nothing there. He knew this because he himself had addressed the envelope, and on one of his afternoon excursions by Southdown bus had posted it in a village some fifteen miles inland.

Few people knew more than Weller did about the gullibility of human nature. Sometimes the extent of it almost shocked him. 'They'll believe anything,' he would say shaking his head in amused astonishment. 'Dress it up properly and some of them will believe anything.' But human nature, he likewise knew, was also immensely curious. Especially landladies and the proprietors of small private hotels. The one certain way of provoking curiosity and having a history attached to yourself was to be secretive. To remain aloofly silent and say nothing about yourself was to invite probing and invention.

When 'Major Charles St J. Weller' signed her visitors' book on booking-in at the Colwyn Mrs Bell had not the slightest reason to doubt the validity of the

self-description. She had even less reason when after
a day or so letters began to arrive occasionally addressed to her new guest. They were letters, the Major found occasion to explain, from his sister (he could
manage a very fair simulation of a woman's hand)
who lived in the country in mid-Sussex. The Major
himself, Mrs Bell further learnt in the course of these
friendly chats, was a widower without any family and
had been advised by his doctor (here he tapped his
chest significantly) that it would be wiser for him to
live by the sea than in London.

'You've got marvellous air down here, Mrs Bell.'

'Let's hope it does you good, Major.'

'Of course there are certain things one misses. In
Wimbledon I used to play a lot of Bridge, for instance.'

'There are plenty of Bridge Clubs here, Major.'

'I suppose there are. You could probably recom-
mend me a good one, could you? No hurry, of course;
it's only a game after all, something to pass the time.'

This was the manner of Major Weller's introduc-
tion to the Fothergill. After his first session there
Weller, who was a connoisseur in these things, knew
that he had struck lucky. The Fothergill was exactly
what he wanted. It was a well-conducted club where
Bridge was played every week day from half past two
in the afternoon until eleven o'clock at night. Like all
such places it was a great haven for men and women
whose lives had become so emptied of purpose, direc-

tion, belief or necessity that they could find nothing better to do. The afternoon sessions tended to attract more women than men; and at the Fothergill the 'afternoon ladies' were in the main extremely comfortably off, not particularly good players and as bitchy across the table as only cards can make people.

The afternoon sessions were the ones that Major Weller favoured. He ignored the bitchiness of the ladies; and the other two conditions were just what he was looking for. Mrs Medhurst, of obviously dyed hair and uncertain age, who ran the Fothergill was constantly having to settle petty acrimonious disputes or endure niggling complaints from members; so that the amiability and pleasant manners of the new member, recommended by Mrs Bell, were doubly welcome.

Mrs Medhurst wished all her members were like Major Weller. If he treated himself to one small whisky at the minute Club bar he invariably suggested that she should join him. If she ran short of the cigarettes which she smoked interminably he was always quick to offer one; he was never involved in any dispute at the card table and was willing to play with anybody, or to stand down, just as it suited the club best. Also he was a very good player.

Before long the suggestion was made—Mrs Medhurst was never quite certain by whom; did she herself make it? Did the Major? Or was it one of the 'afternoon ladies'?—anyway, the suggestion *was* made that some of the ladies who attended the beginners' session might like to invite Major Weller to tea three or four times and have the benefit of some private instruction from him. When the word 'fee' was mentioned in the tentative manner of people who say they don't like to talk about money but who hardly ever think seriously of anything else little Major Weller seemed genuinely shocked.

'Good heavens, there's no question of a *fee*,' he said, 'nothing like that. I've nothing to do. Lots of spare time. And I'm very fond of Bridge. If any member would like a few tips about modern calling and so on I would be delighted to help. And if one is giving what really amounts to a lesson I think it's better to do it at home than in the Club.'

Not surprisingly the Major soon found three ladies who were only too glad to welcome him to afternoon tea and an hour or so of private coaching. One of them, a middle-aged unmarried woman, clearly had designs other than mere card-playing ones. The Major dealt with her in the polite, gentle way typical of him. The second one progressed so well under his tuition that he soon told her there was no point in his coming any more. In any case, as it happened, having had a good view of the inside of her flat, he was not interested in her any longer. It was his third lady, the Honourable Theresa Page-Foley of Wensdale Court, who interested him.

As he explained three days later to the couple who employed him.

It was his second meeting with them since he had been sent down to Hove prospecting and he was now able to report progress. The three were talking in the minute living-room of a small house at the back of South Kensington station; it had originally been built as an artisan's cottage *c.* 1880 and, together with its neighbours, had recently been repainted, generally 'tarted-up' and offered for letting at a rent which its original occupiers would simply not have believed. The woman now sitting on a low stool in front of the electric fire had taken on the lease without a question. For her money was something to spend, and she did not understand talking about it in cheeseparing terms. She handled goods which every now and again brought her in large sums of money and she enjoyed the excitement of getting it as much as the pleasure of spending it.

She was thin and good-looking in a hard sort of way. She was of the modern world, disillusioned, cynical and rootless. She lived with the other man in the room (referred to as Jimmy) but even sex had become largely mechanical for her; it was written up, talked about, photographed all over the place as though nothing else mattered—but what did it all amount to? Not much she was inclined to think. A frenzy and then a feeling of disgust; not much more. Messy...

But organising a coup and bringing it off successfully, that was something else again...

Major Weller didn't like her. He never had liked her.
In fact he was slightly afraid of her. But he respected
her. She was a good one to work with. She knew her
end of the business from A to Z and he thought he
could trust her. He thought that if she gave her word
she would stick to it. '...as you know,' he was now
saying, 'I started giving lessons to three of the old
dames from this Fothergill Club. They all live in flats
more or less in the immediate district. Two of them
aren't worth bothering about. Nothing there. But the
third one, the one I told you something about last
time, Mrs Page-Foley, I think we may well be on to
something there. Have you been able to find out anything about her, Val?'

'Yes, I have, indeed. I think you're bang on target
with her, Arthur. I've found out a lot about her. Her
father was old Lord Arberton who seems to have
owned half Yorkshire at one time. Of course death
duties must have knocked the estate about when he
died but Arberton Castle was absolutely stuffed with
treasures and apparently she inherited a lot of them.
Those snuff-boxes you mentioned last time Arthur,
they were written up in an article in *The Connoisseur*
several years ago and got a rave notice. They were
valued at a lot of money then and must be worth an
absolute fortune at today's prices.'

'Could you get rid of them?' asked Jimmy, speaking for the first time.

'Once we've got them out of the country. Yes. Easily. Through our usual contact. In America, or better still South America, or one of the oil countries—no difficulty at all, if we get the right man.'

'For how much?'

The woman shrugged her shoulders. 'Get the right customer,' she said. 'Get one of the oil sheiks anxious to go one better than his neighbour and goodness knows what they might fetch. It will be good fun finding out. Not a penny less than forty thousand anyway, I'd say.'

'And what's the set-up down there, Arthur?' Jimmy asked.

'Well, this old lady, Mrs Page-Foley, lives in a flat in one of these modern luxury blocks. Wensdale Court. The usual sort of thing.'

'Is there a porter?'

'No. No porter. You press the bellpush of the flat you want and then there's a speaking arrangement to find out who you are. If she's expecting you and wants to let you in she works a switch, or some similar gadget in her room; it releases the front door catch and in you go. You're in. Couldn't be simpler.'

'What about the voice?'

'I don't think that will be any difficulty. This speaking tube affair makes everything sound pretty croaky and mechanical. She'll be expecting me at three o'clock on Tuesday, and if the bell rings then and when she says "Who is it?" you answer "Major Weller here, Mrs Page-Foley" she'll open the door without question. Once you are in you go straight across this little foyer place. Her flat's directly opposite. She'll have the door ajar for you. All you've got to do is go in. What you do then is up to you.'

'Don't worry, we'll see to that all right,' Val put in with an unpleasant laugh.

'No point in knocking the old lady about,' Major Weller said.

'Nobody will get knocked about—not if they behave sensibly,' Val told him.

'What about people in the other flats?' Jimmy asked.

'I've never seen any of them. There must be other people obviously; all I can say is that when I've been there at three o'clock on Tuesday and Thursday afternoons I've never seen a soul.'

'No maid or servant of any kind?'

'Apparently a woman comes every morning for an hour and a half. I suppose she does some housework and possibly gets the lunch ready. That's all.'

'Otherwise the old girl is on her own?'

Major Weller nodded and said, 'She's a pretty tough old character, Jimmy.'

'She'll need to be,' the woman said, 'if she doesn't do what she's told. Where are these snuff-boxes exactly?'

'In a glass-topped case, more or less in the middle of the room. You'll see them at once.'

'And how many did you say? Forty-two?'

Major Weller nodded.

'They won't take up a lot of room,' Val went on reflectively, 'but they'll need to be wrapped up carefully. They mustn't be chipped at all, half the value will go if they are. We shall want plenty of tissue paper. It will take a bit of time.'

'What about parking?' Jimmy asked.

'There is a forecourt to the block of flats.'

Jimmy shook his head. 'Too dangerous. Might get shut in.'

'As far as I can see you can park in the road.'

'No double lines?'

'No, that's OK,' Major Weller said. 'But something has cropped up lately,' he said. Both Jimmy and the woman were alerted at once.

'What's that?'

'Her nephew. Lives in London apparently. She whistled him up out of the blue to make up a four last Friday. He looks as though he would be a pretty useful customer in a scrap.'

'And he is likely to be there next Tuesday?' the woman asked.

Again Major Weller shook his head. 'I can't say it's one hundred per cent "no",' he said, 'but as far as I could make out it's highly unlikely. He comes down to see her very seldom—at a guess I'd say he was scared of the old girl—and when he does come it seems to be always at the week-end.'

'All right then,' the woman said. 'So what are we worrying about? Tuesday it is. And forty forty twenty, like we agreed. Your cut is twenty per cent, Arthur. As soon as ever I've sold the stuff I'll see you get yours. If we get the forty thousand I'm expecting for the snuff boxes you won't do badly, will you? Now let's have a look at the map and you can show us exactly where Wensdale Court is. Are you going back to Hove this evening, Arthur?'

'No. I'm going down to the country for a couple of days.'

'Be careful not to say anything.'

'I'm not a complete b.f.,' Major Weller answered, speaking almost testily for once. 'That's the last thing in the world that I'd be likely to do.'

It was the last thing in the world that he was likely to do for a reason which his two working associates might have found difficult to understand. They knew Arthur Walker as one of the best con men in the business—quiet, unassuming and with a marvellous talent for worming his way into the confidence of rich old ladies. He was so good in the role that it was a pleasure to watch him performing. When they wanted him for a job they knew how to make contact with him in the intricate network of sub-fusc London; when a job was done and he had taken his agreed cut they didn't care what happened to him. Arthur Walker didn't want them to worry about his private life. He didn't want to mix *that* world with *this*. In the Smoke, in the house close to South Ken station, in the sometimes amusing, sometimes dangerous affairs which stemmed from such places, he was in *that* world; when he stepped off the train at Beaconsfield and walked the mile and a half to Rookery Lane he was in *this*.

He turned off the main road into the narrow still unspoilt lane and was delighted, as always, by the rich rank hedge-side grass and the darkness of the over-hanging trees. Rookery Lane had altered very little since he had first taken Molly to live there, in Magpie Cottage, nineteen years ago. Things had been different then, of course. Very different indeed. For the first few years they had only just managed to get by. There had been very little butter, and no jam at all on the bread. But even in the sparse years Magpie Cottage had always been the perfect place for Molly. Just as Arthur was the perfect husband. Not only did he love her truly and faithfully, as she loved him, but he had managed to raise a mortgage sufficient to buy the cottage which from the moment she first saw it, half-hidden among the trees, she knew she must have. 'Well, we can manage, darling, but there won't be much over,' Arthur said. There was very little over, but somehow it didn't matter.

'And old Sir Lucien will give me a rise sometime, I expect,' Arthur said.

'Old Sir Lucien,' the head of the long established firm of solicitors in which Arthur was a clerk, was not good at giving rises. He had a great deal of money, but never saw any reason why everybody in his employ shouldn't manage on very little. Scarcely a year after they were married their first, and only, child was born; a daughter; monstrously spoilt by them both: very early on nicknamed, by now they scarcely remembered why, The Piglet, and the completion of Molly's happiness in life. A cottage of their own; a husband who loved her; a daughter who was the apple of her eye. These were riches indeed, and wiser than many, she had the sense to know it.

The time came when Arthur could reasonably expect, and did expect, the long awaited rise in salary. That evening he told his first deliberate lie to his wife. He simply had not the courage to hurt her by telling her the truth.

'Oh darling,' Molly cried, delighted by his deceitful news. 'I knew you'd get it. What a clever husband I've got.'

'What I'm going to do,' her clever husband said, 'is to put all the extra into paying off the mortgage; and for ordinary expenses we'll just go on as we are for the time being.'

Molly agreed enthusiastically.

What Sir Lucien, always tardy when it came to releasing hard cash, had actually said was:

'You're doing pretty well with us, Walker. In fact, very well. But you mustn't expect the fruit to fall off the tree all at once, you know. For the present I am going to show my good opinion of you by increasing your responsibilities and after a year, or eighteen months maybe, we'll have a look at the money side of it.'

That was the beginning of trouble—or the beginning of real success, according to the way you looked at it—for Arthur Walker.

Sir Lucien suffered, as many men do, from the delusion that he was a good judge of character. And up to a certain point he was. His way of increasing the responsibilities of his subordinate was to say to him, 'You seem to get on well with the old ladies, Walker; you had better deal with Mrs Goldblatt. I don't have to tell you that she's a nuisance, she'll come in plaguing you with questions in and out of season. Just be polite to her and keep her happy. Of course if she *insists* on seeing me you'll have to send her in, but I expect you'll be able to cope with her most of the time, and I certainly don't want to be worried by her if it can be avoided.'

It was avoided. Mrs Goldblatt, a rich, credulous and grasping widow, was so charmed by the polite attention her generally stupid queries received from 'young Mr Walker' that she declared herself perfectly satisfied and never asked to see Sir Lucien again. When, after a number of years, Mrs Goldblatt died the satisfaction she had expressed was not echoed by the executors of her estate. They had been under the impression that the old girl had a considerable sum of money but between eight and ten thousand pounds of it seemed to have disappeared. A lot of awkward questions were asked but they were never satisfactorily answered, partly because Arthur Walker had carried out his series of frauds cleverly, partly because Sir Lucien didn't want awkward questions answered. The very last thing he wanted was a scandal with the name of the firm exposed in the law courts. The missing money was mysteriously 'found' and paid into Mrs Goldblatt's estate and Arthur Walker was given the sack.

'Don't imagine that you will ever get another post with any firm of solicitors,' Sir Lucien told him viciously, 'because you won't. I'll see to that.'

Molly, of course, was told nothing of this. By the time Mrs Goldblatt died the mortgage on Magpie Cottage had been paid off, a pony had been brought for The Piglet and in Molly's eyes Arthur was more than ever the ideal, not-to-be-faulted husband.

Arthur might have lost his job; but he had acquired two things; a knowledge of how gullible a rich old woman might be, and a taste for an income considerably greater than anything he was likely to earn in his clerking capacity.

Financially for the moment he was in a vacuum. He had lost his job and his milch cow had died. Afterwards, looking back on that period, he sometimes thought what a lucky chance it was that he should have met the man called Jimmy. Actually it wasn't altogether chance. The man called Jimmy, and more important still (because she was the driving force behind all he did) the woman called Val were on the look out for just such a partner as Arthur, somebody known to be bent, but of good manners and capable of pulling the wool over old ladies' eyes.

In the underworld of the Smoke there is a wide-reaching network of report and rumour; and although Mrs Goldblatt's executors, satisfied by the ultimate appearance of the money in full, had never taken the matter to court, it became if not definitely known at least widely suspected and gossiped about through a number of solicitors' offices that something fishy had been afoot and that that was the reason for Arthur Walker's dismissal. The dubious firm who had already defended Jimmy in a couple of matters heard the gossip and he in turn heard it from them. Discussing the matter with the woman Val they both came to the conclusion that Arthur Walker might be worth investigating.

'If he's all right in every other way,' Val said, 'it boils down to can he play Bridge?'

'Bridge?'

Val laughed. 'I've got an idea,' she said. 'Something different. Something that hasn't been worked yet as far as I know. You'll see . . .'

It was in this way that what was to turn out to be the highly successful team of Jimmy, Val and Arthur Walker had come together. The woman was the organising force. '*We won't be greedy,*' she said laying down the scheme of operations, 'not too many jobs. Two a year will do us nicely. That will give us plenty of time to work each one up carefully and pull it off without a hitch. And we'll move about. East Coast. South Coast. All over the place.'

'And you can get rid of the stuff?' Jimmy asked. The woman had spent seven years in the world of antiques before teaming up with him. She laughed at his query. 'The way the world is today,' she assured him, 'a child of ten could sell the sort of stuff we shall be getting our hands on. And I'm not a child of ten.'

'You can say that again,' Jimmy agreed.

Ultimately Molly had to be told that Arthur had left Sir Lucien's firm, if only to explain his now occasional long absences from home.

'I've been taken on by a firm in the City,' he told her, 'involved in a lot of big financial deals and they send me about the country looking at things and making reports for them. It's a bore being away from home, but I shall be making a lot more money.' It was sufficient explanation for the completely trusting Molly.

'Just as long as you don't forget us when you're away,' she said. Arthur Walker was not likely to forget Magpie Cottage and the two women there. They were his life. They were what mattered to him.

Returning there when his work in Hove was finished he knew all the old familiar sensations of happiness and relief. Only Molly was there to welcome him, The Piglet now being old enough to have a job in London where she had a flat. 'But she'll be home at the week-end,' Molly said.

'We'll just have to be content with ourselves till then, old lady.'

'I expect we'll manage. Where have you been all this time?'

'Oh, knocking about. I know it's silly not to be able to tell you but that's the way the firm like it, and of course a lot of these big financial deals have to be extremely hush-hush. Anyway I shall be getting a nice fat commission soon and we'll go off and celebrate somewhere.'

Molly smiled contentedly. She had got her clever husband home again and she was happy.

THREE

HOOKY'S statement to his Aunt that he would be busy the following week-end had been made purely in self-defence. Hove and the old dragon of Wensdale Court were endurable, even enjoyable, in small doses, but he felt that he needed breathing space in between.

In point of fact the week-end looked like being empty and uninteresting, and that after an empty and uninteresting week.

In Gerrard Mews Roly Watkins, always a candid commentator on the passing scene, gave his opinion of the state of affairs. 'If you don't get some clients soon, Mr H, you'll be shutting up shop. Like a morgue these days. What's the matter with everyone all of a sudden? Why aren't they going missing or wondering who their wives are in bed with and all the rest of it any more?'

'As Chu Ling says, the bright bird of adventure has been snared in the net of dull conformity.'

Roly considered this an inadequate explanation. 'I don't know 'oo your Chinese friend is, Mr H,' he said, 'but 'e can't 'ave been round Soho lately. The birds round 'ere 'aven't been snared in no nets I can tell you that; why nets wouldn't be big enough to hold what some of them 'ave got if you can judge by the photos.'

'People have turned virtuous all of a sudden, Roly.'

'Let's hope not,' his henchman answered. 'There's no percentage in that, is there? Virtuous? Well, it's not likely to happen to you, Mr H anyway.'

By the time Friday evening arrived it had become clear to Hooky that the pump of animation needed to be primed. And that, of course, meant the Full Moon. The Full Moon, always known to all its habitues simply as the Moon, stood in a narrow passage way connecting two West End streets. It was very much within the orbit of the theatre world and its clientele was drawn largely from the wide world of entertainment. It was commonly said that Eric, the barman, knew more real life stories of actors than the editor of *Who's Who in the Theatre,* and that in any case what he didn't know he was perfectly prepared to invent.

The Saloon Bar of the Moon had all the necessary attributes to make it a popular place for drinking in— it was far too small, abominably ventilated and hideously uncomfortable.

Three years before Hooky had come to know it the Moon had been a very ordinary pub doing a very ordinary trade; then, for no apparent reason, it suddenly blossomed into popularity; if you wanted news of a fellow actor; if you hoped for a chance of offering a T.V. producer a drink; if you were looking for a B.B.C. ear which could be induced (vodka and to-

mato juice was a useful approach) to listen to what a
good serial on the radio your latest novel would make,
the Moon was your place—or if, as in Hooky's case on
that particular Friday, you merely needed assurance
that by observing the amicable idiocies of your fellow
men the harshness of reality could be kept at bay for
a few hours.

When Hooky arrived—on the early side—the place
was only about half full, but what was liking in quan-
tity was clearly compensated for by richness of quality—Darling Duggie was there.

In his usual place. Nobody else at the Moon dared
to lay claim to a particular spot at the bar, but when
Darling Duggie came in it was universally recognised
that no one would dispute his right to prop himself up
at the far end of the bar against the glass case which
bore the legend 'Sandwiches and Meat Pies' but in
which no one had ever yet seen displayed anything to
eat.

'Darling', of course, was used only behind his back,
and then usually by his enemies of whom he had
plenty. In fact Duggie was amused rather than otherwise by the number of people who would have re-
joiced to read his obituary notice. 'I specialise in
enemies,' he once said, 'friends are so unreliable.'
Normally Douglas le Carre Fletcher Findlayson was
known to all and sundry as Duggie. At various times,
according to the hour of night and the level of whisky
in the bottle, he had given so many different accounts

of his birth and upbringing that nobody believed any of them any more. It was the unfortunate fact of his continued existence and his current activities that were of real concern, mostly to members of the theatrical profession. 'There have been Findlaysons famous for all sorts of things,' he once proclaimed, 'rowing and cricket and being Governors of Colonies and God alone knows what idiocy. I'm pleased to tell you that I am not related to any of them. I'm famous for being the most celebrated queer in London and the finest dramatic critic since William Hazlitt.'

When Duggie spoke of criticism he should have said hatchetwork. His paper paid him a large salary and he earned it by being unpleasant. A role which he thoroughly enjoyed. There wasn't a first night which he didn't attend and when the star of the piece nervously opened his morning paper next day the first thing the poor man or woman looked to see was what sort of demolition job 'that bloody Duggie' had done. It was usually a pretty thorough one. Duggie's editor had realised a long time ago that tempered appreciation was all very well in its old-fashioned way, but that vitriolic abuse served up with diabolically clever humour and sailing just as close to the edge of libel as it was possible to go without actually landing up in court was what boosted the circulation figures.

Hence Duggie.

'Duggie's an old sod,' an habitue of the Moon once said. 'But he's a damn amusing one. No denying that.

Unless you happen to be an actor, of course—and even then it's fun seeing him tear somebody else to pieces.'

Hooky, who took the world in general and people in it as he found them, was always pleased, as he was on that particular Friday evening, to see Duggie lording it at the far end of the bar. The very appearance of the man was stimulating—the flowing check cloak, the huge black cravat, the monocle dangling on a black silk cord, the shock of hair brushed back untidily from the undoubtedly massive forehead; then the venomous little eyes, the squeaky voice, the constantly probing fingers with their black nails—'he looks like something escaped from the Cafe Royal of 1908,' someone had once said. 'You expect to see Oscar running after him making indecent signs—if Oscar could run.' All the same Hooky was mildly surprised to see him there since it was the first night of a star-studded revival in the West End; in fact as Hooky came into the bar Duggie was explaining to the little circle of sycophants and baiters who surrounded him just why he was not in the theatre.

'Never in my life,' he declared, 'will I again attend a performance of *Earnest*. That frightful screeching "in a handbag" business. Trying to out-do Edith Evans. And look at the cast they have dragged together. Star-studded? Star-studded my arse! There aren't any stars today only bleeping little satellites. *Bleep-bleep, bleep-bleep*. The one great mercy is that they haven't been taught how to project their voices, so happily you can't hear them beyond the first three rows of the stalls. The divine attribute of inaudibility. It ought to be bestowed by a kindly providence on all prima donnas, politicians and preachers. Have you ever thought, Hefferman, what improvement you would like to make to the human body if you had the job of redesigning it?'

'I suppose a spare joy-stick wouldn't be a bad idea.'

'Ah, you professional lechers, always thinking of one thing aren't you? No. When they had man on the assembly line what they—and who the devil "they" are I really couldn't tell you, but that's the way we talk, isn't it?—what they ought to have done was to include a pair of ear-flaps. If you don't like what you're looking at, and heaven knows that happens often enough, you can at least shut your eyes. Pull down your eye-lids and shut it out. What a mercy if, when the club bore is droning on, you had a couple of ear-flaps you could pull down.'

The Moon began to fill up. The circle round Darling Duggie increased, everyone hoping to pick up some barbed bon-mot which he could quote, or better still reproduce on his own, at the next dinner party. Hooky hovered on the fringe of things; the puppet world with its heavy lacing of homosexuality was not really his environment but he found it—as indeed he found all manifestations of human activity—fascinating to watch.

Eric the barman watched it, too. He knew them all. About many of them he knew things they wouldn't want made public. He was a small, dark man who kept his domain and his person fanatically clean. Dirt offended him. Every time he caught a glimpse of Duggie's black fingernails he shuddered. He served the drinks they ordered with speed and efficiency, all the time the suspicion of a smile on his face and his ears cocked to catch the latest bit of scandalous gossip.

Duggie was not in particularly good form. Tonight his witticisms were mechanical and quite a few of them had been heard before. Watching him from the fringe of the circle Hooky saw the man in an unguarded moment suddenly look much older and for an instant a terrible emptiness showed in his face. Moved by the odd telepathy of such things Duggie raised his eyes to meet Hooky's and signalled to him to come nearer.

'What have you been doing with yourself Hefferman?' he asked.

'Playing Bridge with my Aunt in Hove.'

'Bridge! That last infirmity of feeble minds! And at Hove! I thought better of you. Christ, these people here bore me tonight. Do you ever get that bored, empty, tired of it all feeling? *Déjà vu. Déjà* bloody *vu*. A desolate wind howling in a black wilderness that's all it is. The mistake was giving man a brain, that's what undoes us. Look at this lot twittering around here. No brains, so they're as happy as sparrows. Do you know the Birleys?'

'Boxer Birley?'

'The Right Honourable Richard Studdington Birley, a member of Her Majesty's Privy Council.'

'I was at Eton with him.'

'Then you can come to their party with me. I don't want to go alone. There'll be scores of people there. Hundreds probably. It will be a rout, my dear boy, no less. And I'm tired of routs. I'm tired of the whole bloody thing. Tired of being alone.'

The Birley parties were famous as Duggie had rightly said. There would be scores of people there—the more the merrier—and Hooky had no qualms about adding to their number. Eric, always professionally alert in these matters, became aware that his star customer was about to go.

'That will be one eighty then, Mr Findlayson,' he said.

Duggie looked at him with a splendidly simulated expression of pained surprise.

'What the devil are you bleating about?' he demanded. 'One eighty? You can't seriously expect me to be bothered by all these little dribs and drabs; and decimals at that. Put it on the slate, my dear boy, put it on the slate, and let me hear about it when it adds up to something worth paying. Or better still,' he flung over his shoulder on his way to the door, 'let one of this lot settle it for me, God knows most of them owe it me twenty times over.'

As this was quite a usual way for Duggie to make his exit nobody in the Moon was worried by it, least of all Eric who pencilled 1.80 at the bottom of an already impressive list of figures and went on with his work.

A taxi was passing as the two men emerged into the street; they were no sooner seated in the cab than Duggie was complaining angrily about the antiquated and dirty state of the interior. Hooky listened amused, thinking that complaints came oddly from a man who was reputed to think one bath a week was more than sufficient, and who, at the journey's end, could be relied upon to avoid paying his share of the fare.

It had been raining and a million lights glistened off the wet pavements and roadways of London town. 'Baghdad on the subway,' Duggie suddenly said. 'That's what O. Henry once called New York. Don't bother to tell me you have never heard of O. Henry. Nobody has except me. I used to think like that about London once. Still do occasionally. Funny thing, you can be old and queer and lonely and desolate and still feel romantic at times.'

Eventually they arrived at Regent's Park where the Birleys had a fashionable and expensive establishment. Duggie didn't bother with subterfuge in avoiding payment.

'Settle with the fellow, there's a good chap,' he said. 'I can't bring myself to pay for a ride in a cab as disgustingly dirty as that.'

It was evident, even from the outside, that Duggie's description of the evening's entertainment as a rout was justified. Practically every window of the elegant Regency house blazed with light and even in the hall the noise of human animals enjoying themselves was deafening.

At the door Duggie said, 'I am the Marquis de Sade and this is my friend Captain Hook.' The manservant who admitted them smiled gravely. He knew his Londoners. 'Good evening, Mr Findlayson,' he said. 'Good evening, sir. You will find Mrs Birley in the big drawing-room.'

It was in this manner that Hooky Hefferman entered a house and embarked on an evening which was destined to have some astonishing results for him.

FOUR

CAROL BIRLEY, short, sharp-eyed, almost very pretty, packed with the dynamic energy of her native Texas, surveyed her battlefield.

'There's that frightful Duggie Findlayson,' she murmured to herself, noting the latest arrivals and adding devoutly, 'thank God.' The point was, as Carol fully appreciated, that whereas it was extremely difficult, if not impossible, to like Darling Duggie it was at least equally difficult—if you wanted to keep in the swim—to do without him.

Duggie was the squeeze of lemon which brought out the flavour; the catalyst almost guaranteed to produce some contretemps or other which would ensure full coverage in the social columns of next day's papers.

Carol (nee Gilderstaun) had come over to Europe and taken a long appraising look at the marriage market. With her father's oily millions behind her there had been a wide choice. Finally she had short-listed three: an Italian princeling who had his attractions, but that would mean living in Venice under the permanent threat of domination by a formidable family; secondly there was Maurice, a French industrialist of immense wealth, but likely, she had reason to think, to be unpleasant in bed; third in the short list came young Lord Etchinghall, an Englishman of impeccable lineage and impenetrable stupidity; there were moments when Carol considered his claims seriously, the idea of becoming titled had its undeniable attraction, but in her shrewd Texan way she had a suspicion that the aristocracy business was a bit *vieux jeu* and that she would be marrying into a backwater. Still, there the three short-priced horses were with nothing much between them in the matter of odds. A difficult decision for a girl to make. At which juncture Carol was taken to Ascot and found herself standing next to the Right Honourable (he had just been made a Privy Councillor) Richard Studdington Birley. 'Boxer' Birley. All the right things behind him—Eton and Balliol—and the prospect of a lot of good things ahead.

His sleepy manner and easy way of talking belied the man. He had a brain and had recently been co-opted on to the unofficial Think-Tank which had the real shaping of future affairs whilst the puppets at Westminster went through their ritual caperings and carpings for the benefit of the public.

It was a day of glorious fine weather at Ascot and the Royal Procession had just driven down the course in glittering sunshine. The sight entranced the girl from Texas. It looked like something out of fairyland. 'You English certainly have got something

there,' she said to the tall quiet Englishman next to
her.

The sleepy self-assurance of his acknowledging
smile she found almost equally infuriating and impressive. Daughters of Texan oil barons are apt to be
fast and decisive movers; within a week Carol Gilderstaun knew a great deal about Richard Studdington
Birley. The consensus of informed opinion seemed to
be that he was very much a coming man. 'One of those
clever blokes who might do nothing, or anything,' one
valued informant told her. 'Got more grey-matter up
top than any two Cabinet Ministers put together, old
Boxer; but often enough just can't be bothered. Get
the right person in the driving seat, as it were, and
Boxer could really go places; end up as P.M. very
probably...'

'And what exactly is the Privy Council?' Carol
asked. Being an Englishman her informant naturally
didn't really know.

'Oh, it's one of those odd arrangements,' he said.
'Sort of grew up out of nothing I suppose; sometime
ago now.'

'When?'

'I'm no good at dates. Five hundred years ago I'd
guess.'

'*Five hundred years!* And who belongs to it?'

'Search me. I think most of the Royals do, and
probably the two Archbishops and the Prime Minis-

ter—people like that. One thing I do know about their meetings, they never sit down.'

'They never sit down!'

'Silly, isn't it?'

Carol was vastly intrigued by the idea of the five hundred year old Council which never sat down; she was also intrigued (if also at times infuriated) by Boxer Birley; if he needed somebody in the driving seat to steer (goad?) him into the highest political post of all she saw herself as ideally suited for the job.

They were married at St. George's, Hanover Square, six months after meeting at Ascot.

The girl from Texas threw herself into the social-political scene with immense gusto. Old, hackneyed, and cliché-ridden the whole business might be, but it was entirely new to her and she enjoyed every minute of it. At times she came up against taboos and un-written codes which baffled and infuriated her and made her think that she would never really under-stand the English, least of all the polite sleepy man she had married.

'What the hell gives with these people?' she angrily demanded of a compatriot. 'What makes them tick? *Do* they tick?'

'Ever been to Lord's?'

'The House of Lords?'

'No, Lord's. The cricket place.'

'Should I have been?'

'It's instructive—in a way.'

There was always a willing escort ready to take the much-talked about Mrs Birley anywhere. One was found to take her to Lord's. They sat together from two in the afternoon until half past six watching a dour battle between two uninspired batsmen whose sole object (successfully achieved) was survival and a succession of average quality bowlers who got no help from the pitch. Carol's companion (an aficionado) watched the drawn out contest with absorbed concentration; she watched it, and him, in exasperated bewilderment. He didn't speak much but in mid-afternoon he broke a long silence.

'Fascinating, isn't it?' he said.

The astonishing word almost deprived Carol of speech, but after a pause she managed (one eye on the clock) to ask, 'How long does this go on for?'

'Three days.'

'*Three days!*'

'Five, if it's a Test Match, of course.'

There was an interlude whilst drinks were brought on to the field and Carol's escort became positively loquacious, and as far as Carol was concerned pretty well incomprehensible.

'One doesn't want to speak out of turn,' he said, 'and of course nobody ever knows who it will be. It entirely depends on the retiring President. It's a self-perpetuating oligarchy, rather like the Jockey Club used to be. Good thing, too, in my opinion; that's the way things ought to be arranged. As I say nobody really knows, of course, but one hears rumours. And nobody would be at all surprised if it were your husband. Ah, drinks are over. I wonder if the spinners will come on now, I think they might begin to find something, just a little, in the wicket. And if Boxer did get it I think everyone would be delighted. I'm sure you would be, wouldn't you?'

'If Boxer got what?'

'Why, what I've been talking about—if he becomes the next President of the M.C.C.'

'Is that an honour or something?'

A shade passed over the Englishman's face. History was not his strong point, but he realised now that the American War of Independence had been a good thing... for God's sake let them be independent, he thought, we don't want them...

'It's something Boxer would like to be is it?' Carol, now quite interested, insisted.

'Every Englishman would like to have it carved on his tombstone,' her escort assured her solemnly.

'And does this President of whatever-it-is get paid?'

The Englishman shuddered slightly. 'Not yet,' he said. 'Thank God.'

That evening the Birleys were dining alone at home, by no means a common occurrence with them. 'Is it true you are going to be the next President of this thing called M.C.C.?' Carol asked.

Her husband lowered his soup spoon in alarm.

'My dear girl, we really mustn't talk about that. I haven't the vaguest idea. And why should it be me? Heavens, think of all the men better qualified than I am.'

'But would you like to be, Boxer?'

'*Ça va sans dire*. Naturally I should like it.'

'I'd better start rooting for you, then.'

For the first time in her knowledge of him Carol Birley saw her husband knocked off balance. He was genuinely alarmed and disturbed.

'My God, Carol, you mustn't dream of doing anything of the sort. Not one single word about it to anybody, my dear, *please*.'

'But if it's something you want—'

'Look, Carrie, if ever I am in line to be P.M.— which I might be some day—you can do all the rooting you are so capable of; I'll be glad of it. But for something that really counts, like President of the M.C.C. you must—and I repeat a word I don't like using—you *must* not say a single word to anyone.'

Carol had wanted to ask what M.C.C. stood for, but she was now too cross to do so; she contented herself with saying sourly, 'You Englishmen really are extraordinary. No wonder you lost your Empire.'

She did not visit Lord's again, and if cricket was ever mentioned in her hearing she immediately ruled it out as a topic of conversation. Not that the three day *tableaux* more or less *vivants* of Lord's were every likely to be high on the list of discussable subjects at the house in Regent's Park where the pot boiled furiously round politics, the theatre, the world of T.V. and radio, the latest pictures showing in the galleries, and whoever the current person making the headlines might be.

Now, watching the two latest arrivals, she asked her husband:

'Who's that man with Darling Duggie?'

Boxer looked across the crowded room and flicked over a page or two of memory. He smiled slightly.

'Fellow called Hefferman. Hooky Hefferman. He was at Eton with me. I didn't know you knew him.'

'I don't. I suppose Duggie just brought him along; although he doesn't look like one of Darling Duggie's boy friends.'

'From the little I know of Hooky I should think you could take a fairly safe bet on that.'

Carol studied Duggie's companion with some interest. She saw a solid sort of frame which moved easily in spite of its size and a chunky face which looked as though it had weathered more than a few storms, both material and emotional. 'To hell with him,' she thought, 'I know his sort. He thinks he can get it all by just asking for it. Too easy.' All the same, being a woman, she felt an undeniable slight frisson as she watched the six foot of square-shouldered masculinity making its way steadily towards her. What Hooky saw, as he made progress across the room was very much in line with what he expected to see—a

Molyneux dress worth a small fortune and the most expensive hair-do Bond Street could devise perched on top of a hard bright little face flushed with excitement and success. Being a leading hostess in London had gone to Carol Birley's pretty head as it had gone to the head of many another woman before her... 'a tough baby from Texas, intoxicated with it all,' Hooky thought, 'well, to hell with her...' He was a shade tired of the species; but he was pleased to see Boxer again.

'Boxer, I've gate-crashed your party.'

'What a pleasant compliment to pay me. My dear Hooky I am delighted to see you here. I don't think you know my wife, Carol, do you?'

They became formally acquainted.

'I came with Duggie Findlayson,' Hooky explained. 'He seemed to want somebody to hold his hand.'

'Is that your occupation,' Carol enquired sweetly, 'holding Daring Duggie's hand?'

Hooky thought for a moment about how agreeable it would be to haul her over his knee and spank her tight little Texan bottom; but he answered impeccably, '*Inter alia.*'

'And what exactly are the *alia*?' she wanted to know.

'I make a living from the stupidities of other people,' Hooky informed her. 'You must give me a job some time.'

Meanwhile Darling Duggie, as invariably happened in whatever setting he happened to be, had at-
tracted a circle round him and was holding a sort of
unofficial private court. He himself had once said,
'The only reason a lot of people will come to my fu-
neral will be to make quite sure that I'm dead, thank
God.' The dozen or so people now surrounding him
might be prepared to laugh at his cynical acerbities,
but what they were really hoping to witness was a clash
between him and the author of a play newly put on in
the West End which, in his famous weekly column,
Duggie had subjected to the most merciless ridicule—
including (and this was typical Duggie) a deliberate
misspelling of the author's name which was Anthony
Liddle as Anthony Piddle.

Unfortunately for the spectators poor Anthony
Liddle was no more effective in verbal repartee than in
stage dialogue and the contest was sadly disappointing; rather like watching a cowardly bull in the arena,
Hooky thought—though why the hell the poor beast
should not be cowardly what with picadors, mata-
dors, horses, banderillas, a socking great sword, and
about fifty thousand bloody-thirsty spectators all
ranged against it he had never been able to fathom ...

Encouraged by his opponent's evident helplessness
Darling Duggie was rapidly working up into top gear.
His audience expected a quotable epigram and he
thought it was about time to produce one. 'So much

of modern playwriting,' he pontificated, 'is deliberately cloacal, of the fart for fart's sake school—'

'What a stupid thing to say.'

Duggie was thrown off balance for a moment by the
quietly spoken words. Surprised and angry, he glared
at the girl who had uttered them. Young, self-
composed and yet curiously vulnerable she looked.
Duggie's own youth was now so irretrievably gone that
youth was the first point to be viciously attacked in
anybody still possessing it.

'Ah,' he said, 'we're none of us infallible are we?
Not even the youngest of us.'

The girl flushed a little. 'I wish you would remember that,' she said, 'when you are writing that beastly
weekly column of yours.'

Hooky detached himself from the periphery of the
little group and, with a true instinct for essentials,
made his way towards the buffet. He had rather liked
what a quick glance had shown him of the girl and he
had no desire to see Darling Duggie sail happily into
action with his famous tossing and goring act.

Carol Birley's outsize Texan ideas were evident in
several aspects of the Regent's Park house, nowhere
more so than in the catering department. Her mother
had given her good advice to this point, 'First thing
you do, dear,' that admirably clear thinking woman
had told her, 'is to get yourself a husband who's going places; next, hire an expensive chef, you won't
know what he's talking about half the time but it will

taste good; third, look around for one of those English butlers, Jeeveses don't they call them? Of course, he'll take his cut out of everything, you mustn't expect such a thing as an honest servant, there ain't no such animal, but he'll give the place tone—really good food and drink and tone, that's what you need to get by.'

This trinity of social requirements Carol had very sensibly fulfilled, and whether you went to one of her small intimate dinners, or to a rout served by a buffet table you never had anything to complain about. Hooky surveyed the long heavily laden counter and for a moment almost imagined himself transported into the middle of Fortnum and Mason's. There were exotic things in plenty but he contented himself with a goblet of ice-cold Lanson's Black Label and a plate of Beluga caviare.

'I think I'd like some of that too,' a voice said behind him.

'Why not?' Hooky agreed. 'Simple things are often the best.'

The girl laughed. 'Some simplicity,' she said.

Hooky considered her and found his first favourable impression reinforced; she didn't look like his usual type and yet there was something about her...

'You didn't stay to be massacred?' he asked.

'Are you a friend of that awful man?'

'An acquaintance only.'

The small almost snub nose wrinkled over the spar-
kle of the wine.

'Champers,' she said. 'I don't often have it. Gor-
geous.' Seeing her in profile, as he now did, and hearing her voice again activated a switch in Hooky's
retentive memory. He was not an ardent watcher of
the box but occasionally switched it on to see what
modern playwrights were up to.

'You were in that T.V. play *Bandaberry*,' he said.
The small neat head nodded. 'I was. I don't know why
you should sound so surprised.'

'Perhaps because on the box you looked so much
like an actress and now you don't look like one at all—
and that's meant as a compliment.'

'I'm glad you told me; and I don't imagine you're
in the habit of paying compliments anyway.'

Hooky extended a silver dish. 'Have some more
caviare,' he advised, 'and let it do its mollifying work
before you attack me as you did poor old Duggie.'

'I didn't attack the silly conceited man at all. A lot
of what he says, and writes, is just plain stupid and it's
high time somebody told him so. He just enjoys pulling things to pieces. Isn't this caviare heavenly?'

'Beluga—the best.'

'That's the sort of thing you would know.'

'In a varied life I have acquired a vast amount of
useless information,' Hooky assured her, 'especially
about women.'

'I suppose you think you are an expert on the subject?'

'I am always willing to learn.'

'Not from me.'

The girl extended her glass and said, 'More champers, please, and tell me your name.'

'Hefferman. Hooky of that ilk.'

She glanced up at his strongly lined face, its most prominent feature a large nose that looked as though it had been in and out of a few fights. She laughed suddenly, a clear, pleasant, unaffected sound.

'Yes. Well, that's pretty obvious really. And somehow it seems to suit you.'

'And do I get told yours?' Hooky enquired, 'or are you careful not to give it to evidently undesirable strangers?'

'My name is my Fortune, Sir, she said,' the girl answered. 'At least I hope it's going to be—Janice Mellard.'

Hooky considered for a moment, then nodded his approval. 'A sensible old-fashioned sort of name, Janice,' he said. 'Nice.'

'I shouldn't have thought you would be the type to approve of sensible old-fashioned girls. But in some ways I am old-fashioned, yes. I don't want to jump into bed with every man I meet for instance. I don't want to jump into bed with you.'

Hooky's face creased into an amiable grin. 'A rose is a rose is a rose,' he said cryptically. 'Please don't imagine I'm well read, I came across that bit of Gertrude Stein by accident.'

'I imagine that was the way she did most of her writing wasn't it?'

Hooky replenished his glass but the girl shook her head.

'I suppose you do a lot of drinking?' she said. 'You look as though you do.'

'Beautifully cold this champagne,' Hooky answered, 'funny how important temperature is in food and drink: coffee scalding hot, champagne ice-cold— anything in between is disastrous. And for God's sake don't start preaching at me. I'm past preaching at and praying for. And anyway I've got the great Chinese philosopher Chu Ling on my side. Chu Ling says, or said somewhere about one thousand B.C., that the harsh outlines of the landscape of reality need the softening effect of the mists of alcoholic illusion in order to produce an endurable picture.'

'Nonsense,' said Janice briskly, 'and I hate seeing a man drunk anyway.'

Hooky lit a cigarette, but didn't bother to offer one to his companion. He tilted his head back and blew a smoke ring that drifted lazily up towards the ceiling.

'Now, let me see,' he said at last. 'You're against drink and you don't think much of men—I don't blame you there, mind you, we're a pretty ropy lot of lascivious apes on the whole, but something tells me that starting from those principles and the world being what it is you are going to have a pretty hard job storming the citadels of the West End theatre.'

'It isn't easy,' Janice said.

Hooky studied the young face in sympathetic silence for a moment and then said quietly, 'I believe you.'

A few seconds later he spoke again.

'And from what base is this single-handed victorious assault carried on?'

'You are asking for my address?'

'It's a thing I constantly find myself doing.'

'I'm not at all sure that I want to be added to your list. 3 Lammington Gardens if you really want to know.'

'And I suppose if ever I dare approach the place I'm likely to have boiling oil poured on me from the battlements?'

'It won't necessarily be *boiling*, like coffee—perhaps just luke-warm.'

'I might risk it some day,' Hooky told her.

FIVE

TWO PEOPLE, a man and a woman, sat lunching together at a corner table of the Caprice.

The man, who was grossly fat and whose napkin was tucked under the bottommost of his several double chins, was letting his shrewd, cold eyes wander round the room as though making assessment of the other people lunching there, but his ears were paying close attention to what the woman was saying. He ate very little. Fish ('take that fish away and *halve* it'), a small green salad and a single peach would be a big meal for him; the size of the bill (usually astronomical in proportion to what he ate) never seemed to worry him.

He was at home (if the word can be used in connection with such an essentially rootless person) in most of the capitals of the world—Johannesburg, New York, Rome, Paris, London. They all looked much the same from his point of view. When in London he lunched every day at the Caprice, at the same table and at the same time; and on his English visit he usually had at least one meeting with the woman who was now sitting at his table. Sometimes she had nothing to tell him; but he knew from experience that when she did have anything to talk about it was apt to be extremely interesting. As it was on this occasion.

Waiting until the watchfully attendant waiter was safely out of range the woman produced an old copy of *The Connoisseur* and laid it, open, on the table.

'I don't know if you ever saw this article, Benno,' she said.

'The Arberton snuff-boxes?' The flabby face nodded in suddenly animated assent. 'Yes, indeed I saw it. I remember it well. What beautiful things.'

'They were collected by Lord Arberton during the Edwardian era mostly it seems.'

'Yes, nobody was paying much attention to the things then. Now—' the podgy hands spread in a gesture half Gallic, half Eastern. The thin-faced, rather severely dressed woman was anxious to hear that '*now*—' elaborated.

'Yes, now,' she prompted, 'what would the Arberton collection be worth?'

'Worth? My dear lady, a very great deal of money, believe me. A very great deal. What happened to the snuff-boxes when Arberton died?'

'They were inherited by his daughter.'

'Who must now, I suppose, be an old lady?'

'She is old. And she lives alone.'

'I see.'

A waiter approached the table and Val unhurriedly but efficiently covered *The Connoisseur* with her napkin. When the waiter had gone away again the fat man said, 'And you think you can persuade this old lady to sell her collection?'

'I think I can get possession of the snuff-boxes,' Val said, and for a moment the two looked at one another and smiled slightly.

'Quite so,' the man said, '*entendu.* How soon?'

'I think I can get possession of them almost at once. In the next week or two and I ought to be able to get them over to your address in Paris fairly soon afterwards. Possibly very soon afterwards. That depends on how hard people are looking for them. They might have to come over in two lots. It all depends on circumstances. You know how these things are.'

The large head nodded, the pendulous cheeks shook. 'Yes, surely, care and discretion above all. And I don't think Paris. Not for the Arberton collection. I can deal with them better in Johannesburg, I think. There is somebody there I have in mind. I think he would be very much interested.'

The woman shrugged thin shoulders. 'Planes go everywhere these days,' she said with a slight smile.

'Yes, indeed. And highly convenient it is.'

The woman took a sip of her black coffee and then said,

'It will cost me money to get hold of the things, Benno.'

'Please don't think I am being in the least hypocritical when I say that I am delighted to hear it. People ought to be prepared to pay money for beautiful things. People *are* prepared to pay money for them I'm glad to say. How much money?'

'There are many things to think of—'

'I am sure there are. Think about them.'

'There are risks to be run.'

'Obviously.'

'The old lady is not likely to give up the boxes without—well, persuasion.'

The cold eyes flickered for an instant. 'I have not the slightest interest in what happens to this or any other old woman,' the fat man said. 'That is your part of the business. Please don't tell me anything about it. I don't want to hear it. I don't want details. I want the Arberton collection of snuff-boxes.'

'I can't see that it will cost me less than fifty thousand pounds.'

The figure evidently didn't dismay the fat man in the least. 'Paid in the usual way I suppose?' he queried, 'and on the usual conditions—when I get the goods, you get the money?'

Val nodded and drained her coffee. 'You'll get the goods all right,' she promised.

In the living-room of the small house at the back of South Kensington station the man Jimmy sat intermittently reading the daily paper and steadily drinking. It was how Val found him when she got back from her luncheon.

Jimmy would go for a long time without touching a thing and then was liable, for no discernible reason, to embark on a jag. It always infuriated the woman. She liked matters to be clear-cut, business-like and efficient, and drinking yourself into a stupor didn't make for any of these things. She looked at the man slouched in the armchair dispassionately; lately she had taken to studying him in this way... their partnership had been highly successful she was thinking, but there was a time to end everything and it might well be that the Arberton snuff-boxes coup, successfully brought off, would be the time to break with Jimmy, who was extremely useful in the mechanical part of the operations but whose habits were becoming tiresome.

She crossed the room, picked up the bottle of Scotch from the small table at his side. He glanced up but didn't protest. She put the bottle away in a cupboard and said, 'Don't get started on it for God's sake, Jimmy; not just now. We've got this job to do.'

'You saw him then?'

'Yes of course I saw him. I had lunch with him at the Caprice. I must say you get a wonderful meal there.'

'I'm not particularly interested in your wonderful meal. Was *he* interested in the Arberton snuff-boxes?'

'Of course he was. I told you he would be. The deal is absolutely one hundred per cent on.'

'How much?'

'I said fifty thousand and he didn't bat an eyelid.'

'Fifty thousand quid?' Jimmy said reflectively. 'It's one hell of a lot of money.'

'We can use it.'

'Oh sure, yes. We told Arthur it would be forty thousand.'

'We need never tell him anything different. We employ Arthur, Jimmy; if we give him eight thousand, which is his agreed cut in the figure we first talked about, he'll be perfectly happy. He's got to be.'

The man grinned. 'If you say so,' he said. 'Where does he wants these things—Paris?'

'No. Johannesburg. He thinks there'll be a better market for them there. He's got somebody lined up in his mind's eye already. One of the diamond kings maybe.'

'And what will the things sell for out there?'

'More than fifty thousand, you can be sure of that. But we've got an agreed price and I'm happy with it. All we've got to do is to get hold of the stuff and deliver it. You work that out OK and I'll look after the cash—and Jimmy—'

He glanced up and saw her pointing an admonishing finger towards the cupboard.

'—lay off it till the job's over.'

'All right, all right, all right. Don't keep on about it. Where's that map again?'

The street map of Hove which they had already studied closely was spread out on the table and they both bent over it.

'This is Wensdale Court, here, this block,' Jimmy said. 'I went down there yesterday to have a look round, as you know, and personally I think it's going to be a piece of cake. I will say this for Arthur, he's got a genius for picking the right job. There is a forecourt in front of the flats but, like I said when we first talked it over, it would be too dangerous to leave the car there, we might get boxed in. But out here, Wensdale Avenue it's called, no trouble at all. Park where you like and not all that number of cars about.'

'What did Arthur say about the telephone?'

'It's on the far side of the room from where we come in. On a desk under the window. As soon as we get in I'll show the old lady the knife which will probably give her a heart attack and you slip round behind her with your clippers and cut the telephone cord. Then get your scarf out and deal with her before she starts screaming.'

'Don't worry, I will.'

'It will mean gagging her, of course, and tying her up whilst we lift the goods and we shall have to leave her like that when we leave.'

The woman laughed. 'Well, Arthur said she was a tough old character,' she said. 'She'll be OK don't you worry.'

'Arthur's first class in his line,' Jimmy said, 'his only trouble is he begins to get quite fond of those rich old ladies he noses out and he can't bear the thought of their getting hurt.'

'Arthur will do as we damned well tell him to,' the woman said harshly. 'Don't forget he works for us. We know why he had to give up his job in that lawyer's office; we know he's got a wife and daughter tucked away in the country somewhere that he's dotty about. Arthur will take the eight thousand cut we promised him and not ask any questions about how we got it.'

'YOU'RE just in time to save me,' said Duggie propped up against the bar in his usual place at the Sandwiches and Meat Pies end. 'Eric here is importuning me for money.'

From behind the bar the fastidiously clean Eric protested in mild rebuke. 'I was only reminding you that your account is getting rather large, Mr Findlayson, just in case you wanted to settle it.'

'When you can take time off from making your ridiculous suggestions and attend to your business,' Darling Duggie said severely, 'my friend Mr Hefferman wishes to buy me a drink.'

Hooky felt for that emaciated object, his wallet . . .

'Distressing how second-class minds will harp on money,' Duggie said anxiously watching the barman perform his rites. 'Make that a large one, Eric, and nothing with it.' His hand shook a little as he lifted the glass to his lips but the very first mouthful of the fiery spirit brought the old confidence and jauntiness back into his voice.

'I haven't seen you since we went to that rout at the Birleys' together,' he said.

'I've been around,' Hooky answered vaguely.

'A disastrous evening.'

'I rather enjoyed it.'

'I told Carol Birley when I left that she must be more careful about whom she subjects me to.'

'Come off it, Duggie, you can look after yourself. You're guaranteed to tear anyone to tatters in two minutes if you really get going in vitriolic top gear.'

Duggie smiled complacently. 'All compliments thankfully received,' he said, 'and it is perfectly true that I have at my command the finest stream of alliterative invective since Rabelais but I strongly object to a chit of a girl interrupting me in full flow and telling me I am talking nonsense. Did you hear her?'

'Distinctly. And do you know what I thought, Duggie?'

'Tell me—unless it's something unpleasant.'

'I thought: the finest dramatic critic since William Hazlitt is getting his come-uppance for once. I remembered my classical education, Duggie. I remembered *ex ore infantium*.'

'Oh you did, did you?' Darling Duggie said, slightly abashed. 'Well as you evidently do intend to be unpleasant I'll let you buy me another drink to make up for it.' He pushed his glass forward.

'Another brandy for Mr Findlayson,' Hooky said. Duggie sipped; rolled the comforting stuff round his mouth; and swallowed.

'I wonder who she was,' he said.

'Janice Mellard, a rising young actress,' Hooky told him and instantly regretted it.

'Is she indeed? Janice Mellard? Never heard of her. One of the optimistic sausages turned out annually by the dramatic schools I suppose. A rising young actress, eh?' Duggie gave his high pitched little giggle. 'Wait till I see her acting in anything, by God I'll do my best to see she doesn't rise any further.'

'You're an unprincipled old sod,' Hooky said not very amiably.

Darling Duggie nodded affirmation. 'You're right in every particular,' he agreed. 'It's a pleasure to hear language so economically and accurately used.'

'If ever you see Janice Mellard acting in anything at least you give her a fair crack of the whip.'

Duggie looked up in surprised amusement. 'Don't tell me you are interested in the wench?' he asked.

The truth was that Hooky had become interested in the wench; and he was still at the state of being surprised by that fact and trying, unsuccessfully, to understand it. In his day Hooky Hefferman had had a lot of fun with a lot of girls. They had all been different—surely, they must have all been different he thought looking back on them; tall; short; dark; fair; willing; rather more than willing; all different, yet in a way all very much the same; fun to dance with; fun to dine with, fun to take home to bed—but Janice Mellard *was* different ...

3 Lammington Gardens (when he called there two days after the Birley party) turned out to be a flat in what, to judge from the majority of the population, were the equatorial regions of Earls Court:

'No boiling oil?' he enquired.

'Not today. Coffee or there is some whisky, if you want it. Actually I'm just making coffee for myself. Come in.'

As coffee was being made Hooky opted for it.

The flat was in effect a bed-sitter with a cupboard (the kitchen) leading off it. From the cupboard delicious smells of coffee were wafted into the room. Presently Janice emerged with the coffee and it tasted as good as it smelt.

'You certainly know how to make coffee,' Hooky congratulated her. 'It's an art.'

'One of my few accomplishments,' she said.

Thinking back on the visit when he returned to Gerrard Mews Hooky found it difficult to remember exactly what they had found to talk about so easily and pleasantly for an hour and a half.

'It's frightfully small of course,' Janice had said, 'but it suits me. And out of my window I can see a tree, look.'

The window of the flat looked out on a strip of garden. A small, sad, neglected place. Grimy London walls; an oblong of unkempt grass; a tree. 'A *prunus,*' Janice said. 'In the spring it will be covered in white blossom.'

Unashamedly curious Hooky made a tour of the room, examining with interest the books on the shelves and the photographs on the walls.

'Mother, and self on pony,' Janice explained, 'when considerably smaller.'

'You're not actually enormous now.'

'I probably would be if I didn't diet.'

'And you're all on your own here, leading your strictly virtuous and sober life?'

Janice laughed happily. 'You ought to try it some day, Hooky,' she said, 'it would be a lovely change for you.'

He had gone away from that first visit half intrigued, half exasperated. Next day he rang her up. 'What do sober and strictly virtuous people do for amusement?' he enquired. She hesitated for a second, assessing this unannounced voice out of the blue, then she said:

'My number isn't in the book, how did you get it?'

Hooky laughed. 'You have a telephone,' he reminded her, 'and it stands on a small table beneath the window which looks out on to that famous tree of yours. On the instrument is written your number, it's a habit the G.P.O. has. Whilst you were talking about the glories of your tree I was memorising your telephone number. That's the way Private Investigators behave, I'm afraid.'

A moment's silence, then, 'In answer to your query, walk in Richmond Park.'

'*Walk?*'

'You place one foot in front of the other and carry on like that—you must have heard about it, Hooky.'

'I'll pick you up at two o'clock, OK?'

'I should absolutely love it.'

'Two. On the dot. Ready to start, no twenty minutes hanging about whilst you make yourself beautiful—you don't need to anyway.'

'You pay the nicest compliments in the rudest possible way.'

Hooky's tone of alarm when he echoed the word '*walk?*' had been simulated. He was an energetic type and he needed exercise. On two evenings every week he took himself to Joe Barker's Gymnasium and Physical Training Academy, a somewhat broken-down and dilapidated establishment in a mews off the Edgware Road where Joe Barker, a broken-down and dilapidated ex-pugilist, put him through his paces.

'Ah Mr 'efferman,' Joe frequently said, 'if you'd of come to me before I let the beer get at me and if you'd only give your mind to it properly I could of make something of you; it's a pleasure to see you strip.'

'That's what the bishop told the actress, Joe,' Hooky told him. 'Come on, get those gloves on.'

So the afternoon walking in Richmond Park was a huge success. 'What a marvellous place,' Hooky cried after they had been walking vigorously for half an hour. 'Do you know all the time I've lived in London I've never been here before.'

'What on earth do you do with yourself all the time?'

'My dear girl, there are plenty of things to do in London besides walking in Richmond Park.'

'Nothing half so nice, though.'

Hooky was inclined to agree with her.

'What you said about "private investigator" did you mean that? Is that what you do?'

'Intermittently. Things tend to come and go a bit. More go than come at the moment. But that's the nub of it, yes. H.H. Hefferman Esquire. Private Investigator. Every sort of Confidential Enquiry undertaken.'

'It must be rather exciting.'

A few days later Hooky found himself to his astonishment rowing on the Serpentine.

'If you're really keen on exercise it's a wonderful way of taking it,' Janice assured him. 'You can row and I'll say my part in this rather sordid T.V. play they want me to be in. I only hope your friend Darling Duggie doesn't see me in it, he'd flay me alive.'

'Duggie's not exactly my friend—'

'Of course he is. Two of a kind. Rogues and vagabonds, but I must say I rather like rogues and vagabonds. Not Darling Duggie though; he's just horrible. Of the slime, slimy. I suppose you can ride?'

'Horses are very dangerous animals,' Hooky said cautiously.

Janice laughed. 'Everything's a bit dangerous if it comes to that,' she said. 'We might go out together some day...'

Hooky began to wonder what was happening to him. Areas of innocent amusement and recreation which he had long since forgotten about were being rediscovered. He was aware of curious changes within himself. Other people noticed them too. Roly Watkins, his stalwart henchman in Gerrard Mews, said to him one afternoon, 'You all right then, Mr H? You 'aven't been looking quite yourself these days, some'ow.'

'I'm leading a sober and virtuous life Roly.'

Roly was instantly alarmed. 'My Gawd, Mr H,' he cried, 'what d'you want to start doing a thing like that for? Sober and virtuous? That's right off your line, that is. No wonder you've been looking a bit funny lately. That's no way to carry on. You want to be careful. You want to get mixed up in something.'

This stream of excellent advice was interrupted by the shrill insistence of the telephone bell. Hooky picked up the instrument.

'Is that Mr Hefferman?'

'It is.'

'Inspector Dale, here, Mr Hefferman, of C.I.D. Hove.'

SIX

THERESA PAGE-FOLEY moved round her dressing-room making the small adjustments necessary for her weekly Bridge lesson. She moved slowly because her arthritis was worse than usual. To the world at large the stubborn old woman would not admit that she had arthritis. In the huge family nursery where, one of seven children, she had been ruled over by a Nanny of the old-fashioned sort the idea of illness had not been encouraged; it was normal to be well, if you didn't feel well you were not behaving normally, and if you were so stupid as to behave abnormally you were given either a spanking or a dose of cascara and sent to bed until you came to your senses.

Nurtured in this rigorous regime Theresa Page-Foley had grown up into a remarkably healthy woman and had remained so for most of her life; but the long siege of Time was beginning to tell at last and she had lately been finding out what, in a rare moment of weakness, she once admitted, 'When the human body begins to go wrong, Hooky, it's a confounded nuisance.' Even so the word 'arthritis' was not pronounced, to utter it would be to acknowledge defeat in some degree; the most that she would allow was that sometimes she found it a little difficult to get about as easily as she once used it. As she did now, moving rather heavily round the room, altering the position of a couple of chairs, putting the small marquetry card-table into place, carefully shifting the large glass covered case where the famous Arberton snuff-boxes were housed.

As she made these preparations she was thinking with pleasure of the hour that lay ahead. Joining the Fothergill Bridge Club had been one of the most rewarding things she had done for a long time and meeting Major Weller had been one of the nicest aspects of it. Theresa Page-Foley was rather too robust a soul for the tender plant of affection to flourish greatly, but by this time it was true to say that she had developed quite a soft spot in her heart for the mildly-spoken, well-mannered little man who never failed to tell her every Tuesday afternoon how much her game was improving. If this had been only flattery and no more she would probably have found it annoying, but she was aware herself that under tuition her game *was* improving. Major Weller was clear, concise and patient. And he paid her compliments which she found agreeable.

'You learn things so quickly,' he said, 'it's a pleasure to show them to you.'

'Anything that I take up in life,' she told him, 'I believe in doing well. No good doing unless you do properly...'

This was to be her last lesson from the Major and she was worried about how to show her appreciation of his kindness. Money, of course, was out. In Theresa Page-Foley's canon money did not pass, was not even mentioned, between gentlefolk on such occasions as this.

A number of firms in the Midlands and the North of England employed between them thousands of men and women working full time and over-time to manufacture the goods the sale of which would ultimately secure the dividends from which Mrs Page-Foley drew a very large income. Money in *that* context was very much all right; but the mere mention of it to the Major in return for his kind services would be a solecism which she would never be likely to commit. She remembered the expensive Havana cigars of which her late husband used to be so fond and wondered if Major Weller smoked them. It would be possible to find out discreetly; and then, if he did, a box of twenty-five, fifty perhaps, would be a pleasant way of settling things... The buzzer sounded indicating that somebody was at the front door; Mrs Page-Foley glanced at the ornate French ormolu clock over the fireplace and was mildly surprised. It was not yet ten to three, and the Major was usually the quintessence of exact punctuality. When she used the speaking apparatus to make contact with her visitor she started back almost in momentary alarm at the *boom-boom* which barked out of it.

'Are you there, Theresa?' Laetitia Bitterne demanded.

'Of course I'm here, Laetitia. Can't you hear me? Who do you think it is?'

'I want to come and see you for a moment about my pet charity.'

'I didn't know you had any charity,' Mrs Page-Foley said, crisply. 'Is it now nearly ten minutes to three. Major Weller will be here at three exactly to give me my Bridge lesson—'

'I'm sure you will be very glad of that, dear,' Laetitia boomed happily. 'As soon as ever your precious little Major appears I will leave. On the instant. Meanwhile I'm coming in.'

'He's not *my* Major Weller,' Mrs Page-Foley pointed out. 'Come in, then, if you must and be sure to shut the front door behind you.'

As soon as she was in the room Laetitia Bitterne sat down heavily. She was puffing considerably and Mrs Page-Foley considered her critically and without the slightest suggestion of anything so uncharacteristic as compassion.

'You're out of breath, Laetitia.'

'Of course I'm out of breath. I kept ringing for a taxi and the number was engaged all the time so in the end I had to walk here. All the way from my flat.'

'That's only half a mile or so.'

'*Only?* I'd like to know when you last walked half a mile, Theresa. And up that hill, too. It's a great deal too much for my heart, I don't know what my doctor would say.'

'I never pay the slightest attention to what my doctor says,' Mrs Page-Foley assured her, 'and I strongly advise you not to either. Now what's this charity you were talking about?'

'It's for people suffering from arthritis, so I thought you would be interested, dear.'

'*I* don't suffer from arthritis.'

'Oh, don't you? I thought I had noticed a certain stiffness at times—'

'A certain stiffness, as you call it, is not necessarily a sign of rheumatoid arthritis—but I remember you always were something of a hypochondriac weren't you?'

'There is no need to turn nasty Theresa dear. We can none of us help getting old.'

'We don't have to talk about it though.'

'No, no; true; we don't.' Laetitia fanned herself gently. 'Oh dear, how I hate it—not being able to get about and being short of breath and all the rest of it. Now about this charity of mine—'

Her hostess stopped her with a gesture. 'I have not the slightest desire to hear about your charity,' she said in her forceful way. 'I don't believe in charity. Most so-called charities simply amount to doing for other people things they ought to be doing for themselves. But as you have interested yourself in whatever it is I am prepared to believe that there is some element of good in it so I shall write out a cheque for five guineas—oh, no, we can't say guineas now can we? Everything denoting quality has been thrown overboard of course—five pounds then, I can't bother with decimals—'

'That's very good of you, Theresa. I'll send your tickets round.'

'What tickets? I don't want any tickets.'

'I came here to ask you to take tickets in a raffle. They are five pence each, or six for twenty-five pence, so you'll get quite a lot.'

'I shall immediately put them in the waste-paper basket,' Mrs Page-Foley announced. 'I never win anything of that sort.' She crossed to her desk underneath the far window, moved the telephone slightly to one side and drew her cheque book from a cubby-hole. She was still writing when the buzzer sounded. 'That will be Major Weller,' she said. 'You might just make sure it is, and then press the button to open the front door, would you, and tell him to come straight in.'

THE MAN called Jimmy got out of bed reluctantly. It was annoying to feel as though you had a hang-over when you had only had one drink all the previous evening. Every now and again Jimmy felt the necessity for a lot of hard liquor, but for the past few days Val had told him bluntly to keep off it, and yesterday he had actually found the drink cupboard locked. He

had put up with it because at the back of his mind he
knew that she was right; but now, waking up, getting
out of bed, moving about the room in the first tentative motions of starting the day, he was resentful,
convincing himself that if he had had a few more slugs
of whisky the evening before he would feel more himself this morning. *Damn all women* he thought, but it
was an automatic expression of exasperation more
than anything else. Val was good. He knew that well
enough. She had the brains to think up a scheme and
the ruthlessness to carry it out. The Bridge Lesson idea
had been hers alone and it was a brilliant one. They
had worked it now in Frinton, Torquay and Eastbourne, and in each place they had made a very useful haul. The Hove job promised to be the best of the
lot. Of course they had been lucky in finding the perfect third member of the team in Arthur Walker and
he had certainly done well for them at Hove; fifty
thousand pounds Val had agreed; forty thousand as
far as Arthur Walker was concerned ... Turning these
thoughts over in his head, and finding the last one
particularly amusing, Jimmy made his way into the
minute bathroom.

Whilst he was shaving the circular mirror that hung
above the wash-basin fell and splintered badly. Jimmy,
who was highly superstitious, was genuinely worried
by the incident.

A quarter of an hour later, seating himself at the
breakfast table, he announced gloomily, 'It's not go-

ing to be my day today, I can see that.' Val put a cup of steaming hot coffee in front of him and said briskly, 'Don't be silly. By four o'clock this afternoon we shall have the Arberton snuff-boxes and when we've got rid of them we can spend the next six months in the South of France in the sun.'

Her business-like confidence plus breakfast combined to restore Jimmy's spirits considerably; when he had finished his second cup of coffee and had lit a cigarette he said, 'Right-o then. That's better. Now let's go over the plan again—we'll park in that wide avenue as close to Wensdale Court as we can get, and as near three o'clock as possible—we must make sure that clock on the dashboard is right, by the way. At one minute to three we get out and I do the ring-and-speak business at the front door—'

'That's the only bit I'm at all nervous about,' Val put in. 'Your voice isn't much like Arthur's.'

'No. But we've discussed this before and honestly I don't think we've got anything to worry about. She'll be expecting Arthur at three. At three o'clock the bell rings or the buzzer goes, whichever it is. She'll be quite sure already in her mind that it is Arthur. "Is that you Major Walker—"'

'*Weller* for God's sake.'

Jimmy laughed. 'Quite right. Weller. Not that it will matter. "Is that you Major Weller?" she'll say and all I've got to answer is "Yes" and we shall be in.'

Val nodded. 'Got the knife?' she asked.

The man reached behind him and drew out a knife. He could move quickly when he wanted to and in no more than a second the wicked looking point was two inches from Val's throat.

'*If you want that nice soft face of yours carved up a bit start screaming; if not, keep quiet.*'

Val laughed uneasily. 'Christ, Jimmy,' she said, 'you had me scared for a moment. No wonder the old ladies fold up.'

'She'll fold up all right. Fall down in a faint probably. Meanwhile you will have cut the telephone, like we've arranged already and you'll have the scarf handy—'

'Yes, I've got that.'

'And the cord for tying her wrists and ankles?'

Val indicated where the two lengths of cord were.

'Dark glasses?' Val nodded. 'Wig?'

'I'll be wearing it.'

'And the tissue paper for wrapping up the boxes?'

'That's in the car already, and the bag.'

'Right. Now the getaway. You change in the car as we go along and I drop you at Haywards Heath. 4.42 your train is.'

'I suppose we can make it?'

'Should do. You bring the bag with the snuff-boxes in it back here and put it away in the hidey-hole and I'll take the car and myself to Norfolk. You stay the night here and tomorrow morning catch the 9.32 from

Liverpool Street. I'll meet you at Potter Heigham station.'

'You've got the boat fixed all right?'

'Everything laid on. We'll have three weeks on the Broads—incidentally there'll be a thousand other people there as well which suits us fine—and we'll come back here when things have died down a bit and you can start your end of it—getting rid of the stuff.'

The woman considered for a moment, running over all these details once more in her head, and then nodded. 'It ought to be OK,' she said. 'In fact it *will* be OK.'

'What about a drink on it then?'

'When we've finished, Jimmy. Once we're on the Broads you can drink as much as you like.'

Wensdale Avenue, in which Wensdale Court stood, was a well laid-out, broad, tree-lined thoroughfare and at just before three o'clock on that Tuesday afternoon it was almost free of parked cars. As Jimmy would be driving to Haywards Heath after the robbery and then all the way up to Norfolk it had been agreed that Val should drive down from London and she came slowly along the Avenue with Jimmy keeping a lookout for their goal.

'There it is,' he said suddenly. 'That big block of flats ahead on the left. Plenty of room outside. We're quids in.'

'I told you everything would be all right.'

The car stopped and Jimmy glanced at the dash-board clock. 'Two minutes to,' he said. 'Bang on. Sure you've got everything?'

'Christ Jimmy, you are jumpy today. Of course I've got everything. We've been over it all half a dozen times. Open the door and get out and let's get on with it.'

Jimmy released the catch of the nearside door which because of the camber of the roadway swung open more sharply than he intended it to. In swinging open it actually touched, though it didn't injure in any way, a pedestrian who seemed to have sprung from no-where. Actually he had been in the shadow of one of the big trees that lined the pavement and in looking out for the block of flats they had both missed him. The first Jimmy knew of his presence was the sort of 'plummy' voice he particularly disliked saying, 'I wish you people would be more careful in opening your car doors. That's a fool's trick to let the door swing open like that.'

Jimmy didn't like being called a fool by anybody.

'You hurt in any way?' he growled.

'No, as it happens I am not hurt.'

'What are you moaning about then?'

The pedestrian suddenly didn't like the atmo-sphere; he was not a man to get involved in fisticuffs. 'What a pity money can't buy manners as well as mo-tor cars,' he said and he made off with what dignity he could.

Val got out of the car on the driving side carrying the bag and the two lengths of thin rope. She came round to stand by Jimmy on the pavement.

'I told you it wasn't my day,' Jimmy said gloomily.

'Nonsense.' Val sounded more carefree than she felt. She would certainly have been happier if the incident had not occurred; but it *had* occurred; it might have been worse; it was over and with any luck at all nothing would come of it. In any case there was no going back now. The job lay ahead of them and they were going to do it...

'Come on,' she said, 'sound as much like Arthur as you can.' Jimmy studied the metal plate with its slatted grille by the side of the doorway. 'Press and Speak' it said and opposite No. 1 a visiting card had been inserted bearing the name 'Hon. Mrs Page-Foley.' They both read it together and Val nodded impatient encouragement. He pressed the bell-bush and bent forward to listen. After a couple of seconds a voice, distorted by the mechanics of the arrangement but clearly a woman's, came out at him.

'Is that Major Weller?'

Thickening his own voice a little Jimmy answered, 'That's right.'

'I'll press the catch for the door and you can come in, Major Weller.'

There was a click. The man turned the handle of the door and pushed. It opened easily. He shut it behind him. For an instant his eyes sought those of the

woman. Hers were bright with excitement. She smiled
at him and gave another quick nod. Together they
went into the block of flats. They found themselves in
a small circular hall with the door of number one flat
opposite and ajar.

'All just as Arthur described it,' Jimmy thought; he
found it reassuring after the incident on the pavement
outside. He was now carrying, prominent in his gloved
right hand, the ugly knife with its short vicious-
looking blade of bright steel. He took the few necessary steps across the foyer and pushed open the door
of the flat. For a moment he was flabbergasted. There
were two women in the room... It was a point on
which Arthur had been positively certain. *'Suppose
there's somebody else there, Arthur?' 'There won't be
anybody else. You can rule that out. The old lady is as
keen as mustard on her Bridge and on the days I go
there to give her a lesson she just doesn't ask anyone
else. You needn't worry about that...'* Thus Arthur
Walker; it had all been very reassuring and plausible;
but now there *was* somebody else. There were two
women there; the one nearest the door, short, stout,
obviously the visitor judging by her outdoor clothes
and the hat she was wearing...

Laetitia Bitterne simply didn't understand it... the
small inoffensive figure of Major Weller should have
come into the room and instead there were two people there, a man and a woman neither of whom she
had ever seen before; they were wearing dark glasses,

and black gloves and the man was carrying a dreadful looking knife. Laetitia Bitterne had read about things like this fifty times but she had never imagined that it could possibly happen to her; now it was happening and she was stupefied by terror. She felt her heart give a tremendous leap inside her, then uttering a little gasp she crumpled on the ground in a dead faint, her flowered hat grotesquely askew over her puffy face...

Meanwhile the woman who was sitting at a desk beneath the window at the far side of the room began to rise to her feet. Mrs Page-Foley's thoughts were pretty much the same as Lady Bitterne's had been, but she was not the fainting sort.

'Who are you?' she demanded, 'and how dare you—' Her voice died away as she suddenly found herself confronted with a steel blade pushed menacingly right against her face. *'Say one word more and I'll cut both your eyes out.'*

Theresa Page-Foley was a courageous woman but now she was frightened. Frightened and bewildered. Extraordinary events had happened so quickly.... The next thing she knew was that a scarf was thrown round her head from behind, pulled savagely tight into her mouth and knotted at the back. She was gagged. She began to make protesting defensive gestures with her hands which were instantly seized, pulled roughly behind her and her wrists tied.

'I'll get her ankles tied now,' Jimmy said, 'while you cut that telephone, and then we can see about this other old fool.'

A minute later when they crossed the room to look at 'the other old fool' she was just coming out of her faint. Opening her eyes and seeing the two hostile forms bending over her Laetitia Bitterne uttered a stifled cry. It was cut short by a vicious backhander across the face delivered by Val which knocked the poor woman into unconsciousness again.

'Steady on,' Jimmy urged, 'we just want to tie her up, that's all. What with, though?'

'Half a minute,' Val told him. 'I've got an idea.'

She went to the telephone again. She had cut the flex close to the instrument, and she bent down on one knee and cut the other end of the flex close to the wall. She rose up holding in her hands a considerable length of green cord which she now cut once more, this time in the middle.

'Two bits,' she said. 'Not all that long but enough to fix her wrists and ankles.' When the tying up was done Val said, 'Now stuff her handkerchief in her mouth and she won't worry anybody for a while...'

Jimmy ran his tongue over dry lips. 'Christ Almighty,' he said, 'that's a great start, that is.'

The woman laughed easily. 'What's the matter with it?' she asked. She pointed to the clock over the fireplace. 'It's only six minutes past three now.'

'Six minutes! God, I thought it had taken half an hour.'

'Don't be a damned fool, Jimmy. You're losing your nerve. We've tied up two old women instead of one; what's the difference? *This* is what we want.' She pointed to the collection of snuff-boxes in the centre of the room. 'Let's get that lot wrapped up carefully and put away in the bag and then we're off. Nothing to worry about. All according to plan.'

SEVEN

INSPECTOR FRED DALE was a quietly spoken, polite man who might easily pass unnoticed (as indeed he frequently wanted to do) in a crowd, but who became distinctly more imposing when he was sitting in his own office and you found yourself on the other side of the desk, facing him. Then what struck you most was the quality of his eyes. A disconcertingly steady, direct, penetrating gaze had Fred Dale. You got the impression that those eyes didn't miss much.

'...a pretty shrewd copper this one,' Hooky thought summing his man up.

'I rang you up for a couple of reasons, Mr Hefferman,' the Inspector said speaking in his confidential friendly voice. 'First of all Mrs Page-Foley asked me to; her own telephone was cut in the affair yesterday and it will be at least a day, perhaps two, before the G.P.O. can repair it; and then in spite of what she says to the contrary she is naturally considerably shaken by what happened and I thought it probably best if I got what information I could out of you first before worrying her with questions again. And incidentally Mr Hefferman, if you will allow me to say so, your Aunt is not the easiest person to interview.'

'You can say that again,' Hooky agreed. 'Well, fire away Inspector; but remember I hardly know anything yet; before you start getting information out of me I'd like to be told exactly what happened.'

'Fair enough. Well then, at three o'clock yesterday afternoon Mrs Page-Foley was expecting a Major Weller to call to give her a Bridge lesson.'

'I know Major Weller. I've met him.'

'We'll discuss him later, Mr Hefferman. At three o'clock, give or take a couple of minutes, the buzzer sounded in your Aunt's flat. Apparently she was sitting at her desk at the moment and she asked Lady Bitterne to work the arrangement which releases the lock on the front door. I expect you are familiar with it.'

Hooky nodded. 'What was Laetitia Bitterne doing there?' he asked. 'Was she going to have a Bridge lesson as well?'

'No. She called in connection with some charity apparently. Mrs Page-Foley didn't want her there at that time and told her she would have to go as soon as Major Weller appeared. I gather that your Aunt is fairly direct in her speech, Mr. Hefferman.'

'Devastatingly so,' Hooky said. 'Do you believe in transmigration?'

'Transmigration?'

'I sometimes think my Aunt Theresa must have been a Sergeant Major in the Grenadier Guards in some former existence.'

'Oh, I see. Well, I can tell you this, Mr Hefferman, your Aunt is a very courageous woman.'

'She belongs to that generation, Inspector. They were quite certain they were right and quite determined nothing would make them think otherwise.'

'Maybe we've lost something.'

'So what happened when Lady Bitterne pressed the tit? Did Major Weller appear?'

'No, not Major Weller. That isn't how the thing is worked. Two people came in, a man and a woman. Your Aunt had never seen either of them before. Both wearing gloves, of course, against dabs—fingerprints—and large dark glasses. Dark glasses are a pretty effective disguise actually, it's astonishing what a difference it makes if you can't see a person's eyes. The man was carrying a knife and the first thing was that Lady Bitterne went down in a faint. Then Mrs Page-Foley began to make some sort of protest but it was all over in a minute. The man had the knife at her face—he threatened to cut her eyes out actually—and the two of them got her gagged and tied up. She keeps reproaching herself now because she didn't put up more of a fight. I told her straight thank God you didn't, you might not be alive to tell us about it if you had.'

'Was she hurt, inspector?'

'Not actually hurt, no. Shaken, though; well, which of us wouldn't be? I got her doctor round to see her yesterday evening and he was going to try to persuade her to stay in bed today; but I wouldn't think she pays much attention to doctors, somehow.'

'None whatsoever. What about Lady Bitterne?'

'She's in hospital with a bad heart attack. Whether she'll get over it or not is anybody's guess at the moment.'

'And this couple who came in looted my aunt's flat?'

'Only a collection of snuff-boxes. I expect you know about them?'

'They came from Arberton Castle which belonged to my Aunt's father, old Lord Arberton.'

'And apparently were extremely valuable?'

Hooky made a gesture of half-humorous incomprehension. 'Worth a fortune I'd say. I wonder if they were insured?'

'I asked about that and the answer is "no." It seems that Mrs Page-Foley didn't hold with paying out large sums in insurance premiums.'

'Any chance of getting them back?'

'There's always a chance, Mr Hefferman, and we never give up hope; but this little gang are a pretty clever lot.'

'You know them then?'

'Know of them. "By their works shall ye know them." I think that comes somewhere in the good book doesn't it? Well that's how we know about this particular team. Between them they've cooked up a clever idea, no doubt about that. My guess is that the woman thought of it; somehow it smells like a woman's scheme to me. The way they work it is this: they choose a town like the one we've got here, Hove, where there a number of rich old ladies living alone in flats and spending their afternoons playing Bridge. The first thing is to plant the con man—'

'Major Weller?'

'That's what he called himself down here.' The Inspector consulted a dossier lying on his desk. 'At Eastbourne last year he was Captain Wilson and six months before that at Frinton he was Captain West. The m.o. is always the same. The con man gets installed at some quiet private hotel. We've found out it was a place called the Colwyn here. A woman called Mrs Bell runs it. Can't say enough in favour of Major Weller. Her favourite guest. Quiet; well-behaved; polite; settled his bill on the nail every week. She doesn't believe he could possibly be mixed up in any trouble and is obviously quite prepared to believe the police are persecuting the dear little man for some sinister reason. As soon as the con man is established in his private hotel he asks about local Bridge Clubs. No shortage of these here, of course. He probably had a look at one or two before deciding on the one he wanted.

'He chose a place called the Fothergill, a perfectly respectable club; well-conducted, with just what he wanted, a pretty heavy smattering of comfortably-off old ladies among the members. Mrs Medhurst runs the

Fothergill. Of course we've been there asking questions as well.

'Like Mrs Bell of the Colwyn she's a life-long member of the hands-off-that-nice-little-Major-Weller league. Won't hear a word against him. So polite, so nice to everybody, so willing to help in any way. The truth is, Mr Hefferman, everyone is so offhand and bad-mannered these days that a man has only got to show a bit of old-fashioned courtesy and he's quids in already with any woman over fifty.

'When Weller had been a member of the Fothergill for a few weeks and made himself known to everyone and thoroughly well liked *he very kindly agreed* (I'm using Mrs Medhurst's words) to help two or three of the ladies with their bidding and play. "Did you suggest it or did he?" I asked Mrs. Medhurst. She honestly couldn't remember. It somehow came up in talk she told me and the Major very kindly agreed to it. Luckily for him your Aunt was one of the people who fell for it.

'As soon as he was in that flat of hers in Wensdale Court he must have realised he had struck lucky. All he had to do then was play his cards right—' the Inspector laughed. 'Come to think of it,' he said, 'that's what they call the *mot juste* isn't it? And of course he did play them right. Old-fashioned manners and politeness. One small drink; no smoking; always dead on time. Three o'clock on Tuesday afternoon he was due.

Three o'clock on Tuesday afternoon he came. Apparently that's the way your Aunt likes it.'

'My God, you're right there,' Hooky agreed.

The Inspector spread his hands. 'Well, there you are,' he said, 'it's a very clever set-up isn't it? It's long odds against anybody else being there because at a Bridge lesson you just don't want anybody else; your aunt is expecting the bell to ring at three; sure enough at three it does ring; she opens the door. Of course on this particular occasion it happened that somebody else was there—Lady Bitterne—and she had to be dealt with, but that didn't prevent the thieves from getting away with what they wanted.'

'You seem to know a lot about this gang,' Hooky said.

'We do. We know a lot about the way they work because they've pulled off this particular coup certainly three times in the last four years. And of course we've got a first-rate description of the man calling himself Major Weller. He doesn't seem to bother with any sort of disguise. Last year we put out a warning to a whole lot of Bridge Clubs but—' the Inspector gave a short laugh, 'you go just along the South Coast alone, Hove, Brighton, Eastbourne, Hastings, Portsmouth, Torquay—God knows how many small Bridge Clubs there are in these places; half of them are being run on a shoe-string which means they don't worry much about circulars through the post and in any case they all suffer from what the average citizen always

suffers from and what makes their job so difficult—
they don't believe it can ever happen to them.'

Hooky considered all this for some seconds and,
truth to tell, couldn't help feeling a certain amount of
admiration for the neatness of the scheme. 'And how
will they get rid of the stuff?' he asked.

'Almost certainly abroad.'

'But you can check ports and airports and so on
surely?'

For the first time the Inspector allowed himself to
show a certain amount of annoyance. 'We don't want
anyone to start telling us our job,' he said sharply. 'Of
course we shall check all ports and airports. That's laid
on already. But whom are we looking for? The gang
certainly won't use Major Weller as a carrier, they
know that short of an actual photograph we've got his
appearance taped. It's very unlikely that either of the
other two will actually take the snuff-boxes out of the
country. They'll use a carrier. Somebody there's no
reason to suspect. Any idea how many people use
Heathrow, Gatwick and the other places every day?
To say nothing of Dover, Harwich, Newhaven and all
the rest of them. What are our chaps supposed to do?
Search every single bag, rucksack and car-boot? Rip
open all the cushions? A snuff box isn't a very large
thing you know—' He shook his head. 'We shall do
our best but the odds are against us. The only thing
is—' his voice trailed away.

'The only thing is what?' Hooky prompted him.

'It will be like every other swindle. They'll over-reach themselves. Get too greedy, or fall out amongst one another. Something like that. Sooner or later we'll get a toe in the door and eventually we'll bust it wide open.'

'And meanwhile?'

'Ah, meanwhile. I'm glad you've asked me that, Mr Hefferman.' The Inspector's tone changed abruptly; he still spoke quietly but there was a great deal more bite in his voice all of a sudden.

'I understand from Mrs Page-Foley that you call yourself a Private Investigator?' he led off.

'All Confidential Missions and Enquiries cheerfully and promptly undertaken,' Hooky assured him. 'Any law against that?'

'There ought to be,' Fred Dale said sharply.

'Live and let live, Inspector.'

'Live and let live has nothing to do with it. Catching criminals is a police job. If somebody wants to know what happened to cousin Gladys who disappeared from her home in West Ealing three weeks ago and hasn't been seen since—well, maybe there's no harm in you charging them fifty guineas for telling them you've done your best to find out but can't. But when it comes to villainy, crime, leave it to us, Mr Hefferman. That's what we are paid for; not enough, but that's another matter.'

'So you don't want any help?' Hooky asked, beginning to feel a little annoyed.

'Ah, now you're getting on your high horse, Mr Hefferman. That's how people react to the police. It's how your Aunt reacts, if I may say so. Old fashioned stuff. "I shall be obliged if you would tell me, officer" and "I don't care to discuss that aspect of it, officer" and "if you behave yourself the butler will give you a small glass of sherry on your way out"—that sort of attitude. You say we don't want any help. The police always want help. What we don't want, and what I won't have on my patch, is interference. If you see or hear anything that might lead to our laying hands on the villains who robbed your Aunt you tell us about it as quick as you can. Don't start trying to do things on your own. We'll take all the necessary action. Got it?'

'You're a very forthright man, Inspector.'

'I'm a professional, Mr Hefferman. Thirty-four years of it all told. Uniform branch and then C.I.D. I've seen a lot and learnt a lot. I just want to be left to get on with my job and no one messing me about. I don't believe in so-called Private Eyes.'

HOOKY was admitted to the flat in Wensdale Court by Mrs Perks who on five days of the week came for an hour and a half in the morning to do the necessary housework and prepare the lunch. Mrs Perks was thin and angular and had never before in her life been so closely connected with dramatic events. For years afterwards she would be telling everybody willing to listen, using the modern yardstick comparison: 'It was just like the telly, it was as good as what you see on the telly.' At the same time it must be admitted that Ada Perks, thin, angular and voluble though she might be, had acted with commendable commonsense. At five o'clock on Tuesday afternoon she had been walking home from an afternoon Bingo at the Esmeralda Hall.

'...funny thing, Mr 'efferman,' she told Hooky, 'but I don't usually go along the Avenue past the Court. It's a bit out of my way. But the sun was shining and the Esmeralda had been so stuffy inside, all those people smoking, I thought well I don't mind going a bit far round for once. Get a bit of air. So I turned into the Avenue. Fancy doing it yesterday of all days! Like Fate wasn't it? Going by the Court, of course I took a look at it in passing just to make sure it was still there, as you might say; and at Mrs Foley's bedroom window first thing I saw was 'er Ladyship looking out.'

'Her Ladyship' was the way Mrs Perks habitually referred to her employer; whether this arose from a misunderstanding of the Honourable Theresa Page-Foley's social standing, or from Mrs Perk's own sardonic assessment of that lady's character Hooky was never certain.

'There was 'er Ladyship looking out,' Mrs Perks continued. 'Well, that was a bit funny to start with because your Aunt isn't one to stand at the window looking out into the street, Mr 'efferman. She isn't interested in what goes on in the street. I thought: now when I come to work tomorrow (that's today, of course) she'll ask me where I was coming from and when I say Bingo at the Esmeralda I won't 'arf catch it. She doesn't hold with Bingo, your Aunt doesn't, Mr 'efferman. Bridge, oh dear me yes; not Bingo though; Bingo's common.'

Hooky nodded. 'So what happened then?' he prompted.

'Well, I sort of smiled and went on. I'm not one to interfere; I believe in minding my own business. Only when I'd gone a few paces I kind of looked at the window again, accidentally you may say, and she was still there. And this time I did stop and take a good look. I thought there's something funny about that. It was the way her face was pressed up against the glass and something I couldn't quite make out about her mouth. You know how you get a feeling sometimes, Mr 'efferman? Well, I got a feeling then. I thought there's something wrong. I thought about giving her a wave to see if she'd wave back. Sort of OK, nothing to worry about signal. Only 'er Ladyship isn't the sort of person as you do wave to. So I gave up that idea and crossed over the road and came to the front door of the Court. You know that "press and speak" business, of course. Well, I pressed and nothing happened for about three minutes. That made me sure there was something funny going on because I knew she was inside so why didn't she answer? Then all of a

sudden she did answer. Well, I say *answer*...I couldn't
make out a word she was saying but I could tell it was
her voice trying to say it. I thought *the old lady's had
a stroke;* that's what I'm always expecting to hear, Mr
'efferman, a stroke. I know it will come, it's in the
family. One of my Uncles—'

'Bad luck,' Hooky sympathised, 'but we are talking about my Aunt at the moment—'

'I was in a taking I can tell you. I didn't quite know
what to do. And at that very moment one of these police cars came down the Avenue. You know, white and
blue stripe and a light on top and all the rest of it. I
was out in the roadway waving at them in no time I
promise you. ''There's an old lady in there,'' I told
them, ''and she's in trouble. I think she's had a stroke.
Anyway she can't talk and there's something funny
about it all.'' I will say once they got the hang of what
I was telling them they acted pretty smart, those two
coppers. In the end they got in through the bedroom
window and oh dear, dear me, what they found—well,
you know all about it by now I expect, dreadful wasn't
it?'

'And my Aunt's in bed?' Hooky asked.

'Well, yes, she *is* in bed, Mr 'efferman. And you
know what that means don't you? That means she
isn't feeling very well at all. 'er Ladyship doesn't believe in bed. As far as she's concerned bed's a place to
get up out of at eight o'clock sharp every morning, not
to lie in.'

But in fact when Hooky went into the bedroom he found Theresa Page-Foley thoroughly enjoying her unusual position.

'Come in Hooky,' she commanded, 'and don't be misled by seeing me lying here. Whatever that fool of a doctor may say I am not ill or injured in any way at all. There is not the slightest reason for my staying in bed except laziness and self-indulgence.'

Hooky regarded the tough old woman with admiration. 'A bit of self-indulgence is all to the good sometimes, Aunt,' he told her.

'Well you ought to know,' Mrs Page-Foley assured him crisply, 'you certainly go in for plenty of it. I suppose you've heard all about this ridiculous incident?'

'I've just come from a talk with Inspector Dale.'

'That silly little man.'

Hooky opened his mouth to protest, but the memory of past experiences came to his aid. If his Aunt became seized with an *idée fixe* protestations against it were about as effective as wavelets against the base of Gibraltar rock. He could hardly think of a less accurate description of Detective Inspector Dale who hadn't seemed to him in the least either little or silly. 'I thought he was quite a good policeman, as policemen go,' he ventured to say.

'As policemen go,' he Aunt echoed decisively. 'Thick-witted and pig-headed the lot of them. This man Dole or Dale or whatever he's called persists in thinking that Major Weller was involved in the affair—'

'—But—'

'But nothing. Major Weller is a well-brought up, well-mannered gentleman. When I was young everybody round one was like that but, nowadays, it's a rarity. Whenever I get a chance to play Bridge with Major Weller I shall certainly continue to do so.'

'How is it he has suddenly left the private hotel where he was staying then?'

'Most likely because he is being hounded by the police, by your friend the Inspector, or whatever his stupid rank is.'

'But Aunt T, why on earth should the police hound him, as you call it?'

'Because that is the way they behave. They get what the French call an *idée fixe*—I presume you know what that means in spite of having been educated at Eton—and people who get an *idée fixe* are very difficult to deal with.'

Managing somehow to suppress his laughter Hooky nodded and said gravely, 'Oh, I agree with you there. But just tell me one thing, you say that Major Weller and the other two had no connection—'

'None whatever, I'm sure of it.'

'When the two villains came to the front door and operated the press-and-speak gadget Laetitia Bitterne answered them according to the Inspector.'

'I told her to. I was busy writing a cheque at the moment. I told her to see if it was Major Weller.'

'Well, there you are. She said, "Is that you Major Weller?" and they said yes—'

The old lady sitting propped up in bed sniffed derisively.

'I strongly advise you to give up playing at the thing and join the regular police force at once, Hooky,' she said. 'You would obviously become an Inspector in no time. Laetitia Bitterne naturally asked what I told her to ask. If she had said "Is that you Pope Pius the Tenth or is that you Benjamin Britten?" the person at the front door would have answered "Yes." All they wanted to do was get in.'

'And how did they know about the Arberton collection of snuff-boxes?'

'Plenty of people know about it. Not so long ago there was a whole article about it in one of those glossy art papers—*The Connoisseur*, I think. When you played Bridge that evening here with Major Weller did you think he was a crook?'

'No I didn't,' Hooky had to confess.

'There you are then,' his Aunt said triumphantly.

Hooky knew when he was beaten.

'How is Laetitia Bitterne?' he asked.

'Bad,' the old woman in bed answered with a sort of grim satisfaction. 'They took her to the hospital straight away and she's there still. She had a severe heart attack apparently.'

'I'm not surprised after what happened to her.'

'*I* didn't have a heart attack,' Mrs Page-Foley pointed out. 'What I felt above all else was indignation that that man should have the audacity to threaten me with a knife in my own drawing-room.'

'Yes, well, you're different Aunt T,' Hooky ventured to point out. 'But I do hope that now you are in bed you will have the sense to stay there for a couple of days.'

'I shall do no such thing,' Mrs Page-Foley informed him briskly. 'I have already told the doctor not to come again unless I send for him. As soon as that muddling Mrs Perks is out of the way I propose to get up and this evening you can take me out to dinner, Hooky, at the best restaurant you can think of in Brighton. It's a long time since a young, *comparatively* young, man took me out to dine.'

Hooky shook his head and laughed ... inimitable, he thought, and indestructible ...

'Nothing would give me greater pleasure,' he said.

TWO NEWS ITEMS from *The Times* newspaper of the following day:

'The death is announced of Lady Bitterne widow of the late Baron Bitterne of Iddlefield. Lady Bitterne died in hospital in Brighton where she had been taken suffering from a heart attack consequent upon a raid by armed intruders in a flat where she was a visitor. Asked whether Lady Bitterne's heart attack and her subsequent death from it was due to the fright she sustained at the time of the raid a hospital spokesman said that it almost certainly was.'

'Reports are coming in that a Boeing 707 airliner has made a crash landing when approaching Ciampino Airport outside Rome. There are known to have been some casualties but details are not yet available.'

EIGHT

'FOR GOODNESS SAKE MOLLY do shut that damned door.'

Molly Walker pulled the sitting-room door to quickly, leaving her irritable husband sitting in his favorite chair reading. She herself went unhappily back to the kitchen. A meal had to be prepared for the evening; and, as always, there were various small tidying up jobs to be done—some things to be washed and dried; others to be put away; the contents of the fridge to be checked and thought given to what would have to be bought on the morrow...

These were tasks which normally Molly would actually enjoy doing. Magpie Cottage was her kingdom and she loved to have it shining brightly and running smoothly. But none of this counted for anything if things were not right between herself and Arthur, if Arthur was unhappy.

And ever since her husband had come home, three weeks ago now, Molly had been increasingly aware that things were not right, that Arthur was not happy. He had been irritable and moody, quite unlike his normal self. The Piglet who had been home on two of the three week-ends had noticed it, too.

'Whatever's the matter with Pop?' she had asked. Because openly owning to her fears in so many words would give some sort of added substance to them, Molly tried not to do it.

'What do you mean "the matter with Pop"? There's nothing the matter with him.'

'Oh come off it, Mother, of course there is. Is he worried about money or something?'

'You know I never ask your father about business matters. He sees to all that.'

The younger woman looked steadily at the older one who had brought her into the world. 'Do you think it's anything else?' she asked at length.

Molly Walker's face set in unhappy lines. 'I haven't the slightest idea what you mean,' she answered doggedly. 'Everybody has moods now and again and your father happens to be going through one at the moment. I expect he has been overworking.'

...do you think it's anything else? The Piglet's words remained behind long after she herself had gone back to London. *'Everybody has moods'* Molly had answered defensively, but the words had come from the front of her mind; behind them, in the shadows, lurked the real thought: *every man has lovers...* Once the idea had lodged itself in her mind Molly could not get rid of it. It came back to her again now in the kitchen, where she had retreated after shutting 'that damned door'...*if Arthur was having an affair, if there was another woman...* she tossed her head to

shake away the tears which would force themselves into her eyes and within herself she uttered the age-old, agonised despairing question *what have I done wrong? Where have I failed him? What has he found in her, whoever she is, that I haven't given him?* ...

'I shall be going to London tomorrow,' Arthur announced later that evening.

'On business, Arthur?'

'Of course on business. You don't imagine I'm going to spend a day gallivanting round the West End for fun do you?'

'I just asked Arthur, that's all.'

'Sorry old girl, I was a bit short I'm afraid.'

'That's all right; but you have been a bit short, you know, during the last week or two. Are you worried about anything?'

'What should I be worried about?'

'There's nothing wrong is there?'

'Wrong? Of course there's nothing wrong. What could be wrong? Really, my dear girl, the way you go on!'

Molly was wise enough to say no more; that night lying awake in the darkness a sentence that she had read somewhere about a woman in the New Testament came into her mind 'and thine own heart a sword shall pierce'—perhaps all women's hearts were pierced with swords, she thought...

Arthur Walker, on his way to London next day, was indeed a very worried man. And a frightened one. He had had one single communication from his companions since the affair at Hove; a letter from Potter Heigham consisting of one sentence only, telling him when to present himself at the house behind South Kensington station. The letter had contained nothing beyond that bare instruction; but Arthur had, of course, already seen the paragraph about Laetitia Bitterne's death in his paper and it had most thoroughly scared him. Violence was something he wanted no part in. He had always insisted on that. He saw that it might be necessary to leave the victim trussed up for an hour or so but this Lady Bitterne business was something very different. Terribly different. Lady Bitterne had died, and the hospital had said that she had died because of what had been done to her by the raiders. Dreadful words like murder, or at the best manslaughter kept darkening Arthur Walker's mind...

Murder, manslaughter, accessory before the fact... Christ Almighty, he thought, how the hell did I ever get mixed up in this sort of thing? If only old Mrs Goldblatt hadn't been such a complete fool, so stupidly trusting...if only he hadn't gone wrong then by now he would have a responsible job in Sir Lucien's firm and the dreadful words murder, manslaughter, accessory before the fact would never have come near him...

In the South Kensington house the man and the woman were sitting talking. Jimmy was drinking and obviously had been drinking pretty heavily. He was on the bottle again. Arthur was greeted with a cheerfulness which he instinctively felt to be completely false. He didn't like the atmosphere a bit.

'Drink Arthur?'

'No thanks, it's a bit early for me.'

'It's a bit early for anybody,' the woman said. Jimmy's only reaction was very deliberately to pour himself another slug of whisky.

'I suppose you read about what happened at Hove,' he said. 'What do you make of it?'

'What do I make of it? What I always have made of it. You both know I've always said the same thing,' Arthur turned from the man to the woman for confirmation. 'No unnecessary rough stuff. No violence. I've always said it haven't I? A straightforward con job to get inside and then clear off with the stuff—that's one thing. Knocking people about is something else and I don't want any part of it.'

'She shouldn't have been there, Arthur. You told us the woman who lived in the flat would be alone didn't you?'

'I told you it was almost certain she would be alone. And so it was. When I was giving her a Bridge lesson it stands to sense she wouldn't want anybody else there, doesn't it? But there was always the *chance*, the off chance, one chance in a hundred. You're not going to try to tell me that was my fault are you?'

'We aren't saying it was anybody's fault,' the woman said, 'but it happened. She was there and she had to be dealt with. So I dealt with her.'

'Well, I don't want anything of that,' Arthur repeated, 'I just want to get out of it all now. Give me my cut and I'll go.'

Jimmy took a swig at his drink and said, 'Tell him, Val.'

'Did you see in the papers about that Boeing 707 crashing at Rome airport?' the woman asked.

The question surprised Arthur and he wondered what turn the conversation had taken.

'An air crash?' he said. 'When was that?'

'It was in all the papers two days after our little job at Hove.'

Still puzzled Arthur threw his mind back. 'Yes, I think I do remember reading something about it. What of it?'

'One of the people killed was the South African millionaire the Arberton snuff-boxes were going to be sold to.'

Arthur was jolted by this unwelcome piece of news but said hopefully enough, 'Well, I suppose your contact man can find somebody else to buy them can't he?'

'I expect he can. But it may take some time. My contact had this one particular man lined up for the deal. He was collecting mad and he had the money. Now we've got to find somebody else. And it isn't everyone in the world who's got fifty thousand pounds to spare.'

'I thought it was to be forty thousand,' Arthur said looking from the man to the woman and not sure whether he had intercepted a significant look between them or not.

'It was forty thousand,' Val answered him, adding with an easy laugh, 'What did I say? Fifty? Wishful thinking.'

'And if it is forty my cut on it is eight,' Arthur said. 'That's what we agreed isn't it?'

'That's right.'

'Then I'll take it and go.'

'Act your age, Arthur,' the woman told him sharply. 'There's no cut for anybody yet. Not till the stuff is sold. You couldn't help that other woman being in the flat at Hove and we couldn't help the Boeing crashing in Rome. The stuff will be sold; but we've got to get the right man for it and that means waiting.'

'I'll wait then.'

'You'll have to. And in the meantime I've got my eye on something else. I think we'll give the South Coast a rest and try somewhere entirely different. The Midlands. Birmingham's full of money and mugs. And Bridge Clubs too; must be. If you can get inside one of those big houses Edgbaston way, Arthur, you'll find something worth while, I'll be bound.'

Arthur Walker shook his head.

'Not for me. I'm quitting.'

'You can't do that, Arthur; we're a team.'

'Not any more. This lot at Hove has finished it as far as I am concerned. I don't say I've done badly out of it, but I'm not doing any more. It was always understood between us that there wasn't going to be any violence and now look what's happened.'

'Don't be a fool, the old woman died because she had a heart attack.'

'She had a heart attack because of what you did to her.'

'And if we all three keep our mouths shut tight how can the law trace it to us?'

'Maybe they can't. Let's hope to God they can't. And I'm not giving them another chance after this. I'm opting out.'

'Just one more job, Arthur.'

'No. You must find somebody else.'

'There isn't anybody else as good as you at it, Arthur. You've got these old Bridge-playing ladies taped from the word go. You can get them eating out of your hand in no time.'

Arthur Walker still shook his head.

'No more,' he said. 'Not for me. You can pay me my cut in the last job and start looking for someone else. No hard feelings or anything like that, but I'm quitting.'

The woman lit a cigarette, inhaled and blew a long plume of smoke thoughtfully into the air. 'Arthur,' she said quietly, 'there are going to be some very hard feelings if you don't agree to come in with us on one more job, very hard indeed.'

'I just want to go home and forget about all this.'

'Maybe you do. Just like you've forgotten why it was you lost that good job in Sir Lucien's solicitor's office. You wouldn't want telephone calls coming to your cottage in the country asking about that, would you?'

'Don't you start telephoning me at home or there'll be trouble.'

The threat made Val laugh. 'You go home and think it over, Arthur.'

NINE

In Gerrard Mews Roly Watkins who had come up to see if Hooky would like an early afternoon cup of tea found him packing a small suitcase.

'You shutting up shop then, Mr H?' he enquired. 'Decided to do a flit, 'ave you?'

'Duty calls, Roly. I'm off to Hove.'

'Got a little love nest down there, 'ave you? Something nice and cuddly by the seaside?'

'Does your lascivious mind never think of anything else except fornication and lechery?'

'Not often, Mr H. No, I can't say as it does.'

'I am visiting my Aunt, Roly.'

Roly Watkins became serious at once. 'Ah well, that's different,' he said. 'There's no little love nest there I'll grant you that. You'll be lucky if you get out of the lion's cage alive, Mr H.'

It was three weeks since the robbery in Wensdale Court and Hooky was perfectly truthful when he told Roly that a sense of duty was taking him once more to Hove. His Aunt had proved so stubbornly intransigent immediately after the affair and had shown herself to be so aggressively self-sufficient that he had come away from his last visit there more than half-inclined to let the old lady stew in her own juice. After three weeks, however, (and aided it must be admitted by the fact that business in Gerrard Mews was minimal) he had decided that he had better run down for at least one night to see how things were going. His telephoned proposal was warmly received at the Hove end. 'Of course, Hooky. I shall be delighted to see you. If you have enough sense to leave that dangerous car of yours in the garage—if you *have* a garage that is—and come by rail, you had better catch the four o'clock train from Victoria Station. That means you will be at the flat a few minutes after five.' His Aunt then added a sentence which, in the light of her last utterances on the subject, Hooky found staggering, 'Don't come earlier,' she warned him briskly 'as I am expecting one of those nice policemen to tea. Goodbye.'

On arrival Hooky sought elucidation about the 'nice policeman.'

'Not that creature you got mixed up with,' his Aunt told him sharply. 'Dull or Doll or whatever his name was.'

'I didn't get mixed up with him, as you call it,' Hooky expostulated, 'it was just that he was dealing with the case.'

'The trouble with you, Hooky, is that you don't make contact with the right people, do you? I made it quite plain that I didn't want to have anything more to do with your Dull-Doll friend and they sent out someone else to see me. A Chief Inspector. A charming man. By a coincidence his grandmother was married to the stud groom on the Arberton estate. He has been here this afternoon.'

'To tell you that they are actively pursuing enquiries, presumably.'

'The police, Hooky, have a very great deal to do and in my opinion do it very well—some of them.'

'But they haven't caught anybody yet, or found the snuff-boxes?'

'Chief Inspector Lewis is quite sure that the snuff-boxes will be found in time—provided that the police are left alone to get on with their work.'

'Is that meant as a warning signal, my dear Aunt?'

'Very definitely so, Hooky. Chief Inspector Lewis had heard that you claim to be a private investigator—'

'Not only claim to be a private investigator,' Hooky put in a little sharply, 'I am one. How else do you think I make a living?'

'I very often wonder. And I wonder still more how having made a living you manage to dissipate it all so thoroughly. But your bad habits are your own affair, Hooky; not mine, thank goodness. I am only making the point that Chief Inspector Lewis told me very politely, but very firmly, that this matter is far better left to the professionals and not meddled with by amateurs.'

It was an unexpected reception and after an hour and a half of it Hooky felt that he didn't want to hear

any more for the moment about the sterling qualities
of Chief Detective Inspector Lewis and the troublesome habits of interfering private eyes.

'I think I'll take a turn along the front,' he announced.

'An excellent idea,' Mrs Page-Foley agreed. 'I'm
sure you don't get enough exercise in London. Chief
Detective Inspector Lewis has a dog which he takes for
a walk every day. A boxer.'

One of two picturesque remarks about the Chief
Inspector and his dog came into Hooky's mind, but he
suppressed them; the current mode of uninhibited
speech had not yet penetrated Wensdale Court.

Hooky's 'turn along the front' naturally took him
as fast as he could go to the nearest pub he knew—The
Raven. The bored barmaid was there, reading the
Evening Argus. She looked up, paused for a second
whilst memory did its work, and then smiled.

'You've been in before,' she said.

'Once seen never forgotten,' Hooky pointed to his
twice broken nose.

The barmaid considered his face critically and
carefully. 'Well, personally I like it,' she said. 'I like a
man to look like a man, not like half the people who
come mincing in here.'

Hooky grinned at her. He was feeling better already. 'I'm a mincee,' he told her. 'I've been through
the mincer.'

'More than once,' the girl agreed. 'I'll be bound. Last time you were in you said you were going to see your Aunt.'

'And this time I've just come from seeing her.'

'Is she the mincer?'

'You could say that. I feel extremely exhausted.'

'You're sure she's your Aunt?'

'I need a very large whisky, Teachers, please—with singularly little water.'

The barmaid poured out the drink and indicated the carafe of water. 'Help yourself,' she invited, 'and I'll bet plenty of girls have said that to you in your time.'

'You're doing my Ego a lot of good,' Hooky told her.

'I've never heard it called that before,' the girl said.

This promising conversation was interrupted by the arrival of a second customer. Hooky remembered the cavalry twill trousers, the artificial fly stuck in the tweed hat and the plummy voice which now said, 'Large pink gin, my dear, please.'

The newcomer took off his tweed hat and shook some rain drops onto the floor. Hook had very little hope that anything interesting in the way of conversation would develop, but once inside a pub it was against his nature to remain taciturn. And there was always one topic on which any two Englishmen, total strangers though they might be, could safely and properly embark.

'Raining?' Hooky enquired amiably.

'Just started. What a climate. Not like this in Majorca.'

Hooky recognised the type. The holiday-anecdote fiend. Determined to let everybody know he has been abroad. Capable (Hooky winced at the thought) of producing a wallet stuffed with holiday snaps at any moment.

'You been to Majorca?' the man enquired, but now his voice had taken on a slightly, but unmistakably, different tone. Something had happened to him. Hooky for once was wearing his O.E. tie and little plummy voice had noticed it. He was a man on whom the sight of an O.E. tie had a profound effect. He was quite clear in his own mind that he himself ought to have gone to Eton; in fact there were times when he almost succeeded in persuading himself that he had gone there. Any Old Etonian, he was sure, would rec- ognise him as a congenial spirit. Hooky had been to a lot of places up and down the world, but never as it happened to Majorca. He shook his head.

'Not what it used to be. Dear me, no. Full of the fish and chips brigade nowadays. But then everything has changed hasn't it? . . .'

Hooky withdrew his mind. He found these nostal- gic moaners extremely boring. They all used the same script and he could have written it for them. They had all, apparently, lived in large houses, staffed by the well-trained servants and they had all witnessed with dismay the steady deterioration in manners and standards all round them....

'Why the hell didn't you do something about it then?' he often felt inclined to ask when forced to listen to one of them. 'If your whole generation was so strictly brought up and so well behaved and generally so bloody marvelous, how come you let the world get into the mess it is in?'

It was a question he would have liked to put to Cavalry Twill Trousers, puffing out his cheeks and sipping at his large pink gin; but Hooky felt too amiably lazy to embark on argument; he concentrated his attention on the barmaid and was rewarded with a wink. Hooky, ever an opportunist in these matters, began to wonder whether there might be possibilities here... a bit close to his Aunt's doorstep, of course, but it was always worth taking a risk in a good cause...

'...take cars,' the little man was now well launched on his scathing litany against everybody and everything modern (except of course himself, and the way of life he was able to believe that he lived) 'everybody drives about in one today. Tom, Dick and Harry. Democracy. No manners, nothing. Why just before I went off to Majorca I was very nearly knocked down by one...'

...*Christ*, Hooky thought. A *'my accident'* story *now, with a long account of how brave he was and how well he came out of it all....*

'... in Wensdale Avenue' the man was saying. For the first time since the commencement of the monologue Hooky became faintly interested.

'What happened in Wensdale Avenue?' he asked.

'This car drew up, hard against the pavement, just outside the big block of flats there, Wensdale Court isn't it? naturally the man driving, one of these modern types, didn't bother to look if anyone was coming along on the pavement. Dear me no, nothing like that. In a hurry to get out, so he just undoes the door and flings it open. If I'd been another yard further forward it would have hit me hard, as it was I practically walked into it. No consideration, nothing. I said to him, and you'll appreciate this I'm sure' (a hard meaningful glance at the O.E. tie) 'I said, "What a pity money can't buy manners as well as motorcars." That's the only way to treat them, like the dirt they are, don't you agree?'

'When did this enthralling event take place?' Hooky asked.

'Three weeks ago. The afternoon of the day I flew to Majorca.'

'In the afternoon?'

'Just about three. I had to go back to my place and get packed up and be away shortly after four.'

'What day of the week was this?'

'Tuesday. There's a cheap night flight on Tuesday evenings. Nowadays, of course, one has to go on these cheap flights. It's only butchers and bookmakers, that sort of person, who can afford the normal fare. Still, that's the way everything has gone, isn't it?'

Hooky nodded. 'Dreadful, dreadful,' he agreed. 'So on Tuesday afternoon, three weeks ago, just about three o'clock a car drew up outside Wensdale Court and a man got out?'

'There was a woman with him too.'

'A man and a woman got out. And did they actually go into Wensdale Court?'

'Yes, they did. When I had said my bit about good manners and so on I moved off. I wasn't going to get involved in an argument with people like that. But I did glance back and, yes, there they were, going into Wensdale Court.'

'Could you describe them?'

'Describe them? Why, is there something wrong then?'

'An Aunt of mine lives in Wensdale Court,' Hooky elaborated with deliberate woolliness, 'and she had some visitors calling on that day and she wanted to know something more about them. I just wondered if they were your two.'

Pink Gin thought hard.

'I don't think I could exactly *describe* them, no,' he said at last. 'I'm sure you will understand I wasn't really interested in them. Not my sort.'

'No, no. Of course not. And what kind of car were they driving?'

'Not the foggiest, old man. Simply not the foggiest. If your Aunt wants to know more about them I'd like to help her, of course, but I'm afraid I can't.'

Hooky was disappointed but not surprised. His work as a private investigator had long since made him realise what every professional policeman knows only too well that people see and don't observe, hear and don't take in, experience and remember nothing of. He was used to the fact that a hundred questions, maybe five hundred, have to be asked before any sort of useful answer is forthcoming. But this time he was lucky. The Gods smiled on him. Out of the blue Pink Gin volunteered something.

'I did notice one thing,' he added. 'When I bent down to speak through the car window and tell this chap what I thought of him I saw a what-do-you-call-it—' he looked to Hooky for assistance. Hooky was unable to help him. '—a *brochure*,' Pink Gin went on, inspiration coming to his aid, 'sort of advertisement pamphlet thing in the dashboard cubby hole and I could see the title of it. *The Norfolk Broads*. I don't know if your Aunt knows anybody in that part of the world?'

Hooky didn't know either. Two unidentified people with a possible past or future interest in the Norfolk Broads didn't seem a very promising start to him.

But it was something; and he didn't feel disposed at the moment to share even that something with the professionals who were so definite that they didn't want his help.

TEN

ABOUT A WEEK LATER Roly Watkins made a typical entrance into Hooky's working-sleeping-eating-drinking apartment. 'Busy, Mr H?' he enquired.

'The bird of enormous energy flutters frustratedly in the confined cage of enforced inaction. Chu Ling.' Hooky answered. He was not busy.

'Your Chinese chum certainly slobbered a bibful then,' Roly said admiringly. 'Well, you can stop fluttering and start to do a bit of pecking. There's another sort of bird downstairs.'

'To see me?'

'A young lady by the name of Mellard.'

Hooky's face creased in a happy smile. 'I am delighted to hear it,' he said.

'I thought you would be. Never learn, do you?'

'Stop moaning and moralising Roly and show Miss Mellard up.'

When Janice came in looking very young and fresh Hooky upbraided her. 'Where have you been all this time?' he demanded. 'I'm getting old and flabby. No walks in Richmond Park, no rowing on the Serpentine. My life has been empty without you.'

Janice laughed. 'You say the silliest things in the nicest way, Hooky,' she said.

'I thought you had deserted me.'

'Actually I've been busy. I've had a job, which is too marvellous in these days. Do you know the T.V. series *Willoughby*?'

'One, two, or the unofficial machine?'

'What you call the unofficial machine. Lonny Adberg is producing it and I've got a part—not very much, but still something—in two of the episodes.'

'I told Darling Duggie you were a rising young actress; now you've risen evidently.'

'Thank goodness Duggie isn't a T.V. critic. I don't flatter myself that I'm his favorite person.'

'*Willoughby*?' Hooky queried, the wheels of memory beginning to revolve a little. 'Half a minute, hasn't it been running for some time?'

'Months; I've only just come into it.'

'I think I did see one episode of it some time ago. Isn't it about reasonably well-mannered people who speak the Queen's English and live in civilised surroundings?'

'That's the one.'

'Then it's doomed to failure isn't it, my dear girl? Great is the god of the kitchen sink and loudly shall he be worshipped in the most slipshod and vulgar language—that's the canon today. Long live mediocrity.'

'I don't think you'd get on very well at the B.B.C., Hooky.'

'I sincerely hope not.'

'But I didn't come here to talk about myself.'

'I can't imagine many nicer topics.'

'Do you remember telling me you were a private investigator?' Hooky nodded, watching the young face closely. Young and not yet much marked by life; but Hooky made a guess that she was worried about something.

'Anything on your mind?' he asked quietly.

'Yes, there is, Hooky. I want help. I want to tell somebody about it.'

'Sometimes telling somebody is the greatest help of all. Go ahead and don't forget that a private eye is also a private ear. In the course of conversation you may hear me babble a lot of nonsense, but you won't ever hear me babble about what a client has said to me.'

'That's just what I want to be, Hooky, a client. I want you to help me; but I want to pay for it. It's got to be a job.'

'Don't worry. You'll get a bill in due course. If I take on the job, that is. I don't know anything about it yet.'

'I think I ought to tell you a bit about myself first—'

'I've no objection,' Hooky assured her.

'—just to let you know that I'm not really the type likely to worry about nothing, or imagine a whole lot of non-existent things. Also, I must explain, that although as you know, I live by myself in a flat in London I have a perfectly good home to go to whenever I want to.'

'Do both your parents live there?'

'It may be very unfashionable; but yes, they do. I had a very happy childhood, Hooky.'

'Brothers and, or, sisters?'

'No. I'm an only child and I couldn't have had a kinder or more loving father and mother.'

...everything hunky-dory on the home front, thought Hooky which makes a nice change these days; so what has the girl been up to? Got herself into some sort of trouble? *'Some sort of trouble'* he reflected with a guilty feeling, was another way of spelling man and his never satisfied lusts. He wondered a little unhappily what mischief some yet unidentified specimen of the naked ape had been up to...'

'So what sort of jam have you got yourself into?' he asked gently.

'It isn't me, it's my father.'

'Your father?'

'And it isn't anything that I *know*—and yet I *do* know it. Does that sound silly?'

'Not to me. Carry on.'

'Well, ever since I've been living in Lammington Gardens I've gone home as often as I can. Not every weekend, of course, but frequently. And until recently everything has always been just the same as ever, Mummy and Daddy obviously happy together and me getting on with both of them just as I always have done.'

'Until recently—' Hooky prompted.

'Until about a month ago.'

'What happened since then?'

'Daddy has been a different person. You just can't help noticing it. He's irritable and unhappy; and, Hooky, I think he's scared.'

Hooky studied the girl without speaking for a few moments, and she went on, 'Of course, you can say that I'm imagining it all if you like. Only I'm not that type. And anyway when you really love a person you don't need to have everything spelt out in capital letters. Besides my mother has noticed it, too.'

'And what do you suppose the trouble is? Any idea?'

The girl hesitated. She was essentially a loyal person. Saying something which sounded like lese-majesty didn't come easily to her.

'I suppose it could be another woman,' she said at length. 'Even happily married men do go off the rails occasionally, don't they, Hooky?'

'I've heard of it,' Hooky told her a little grimly.

'I must say Daddy and Mummy are the very last people I would have thought this could happen to; but that's what it looks like.'

'What does your mother say about it?'

'She thinks so, too. Only she won't say so. And if that's what it *is*, then I can't imagine how she'll ever get over it. It's a funny thing to say about people who are married, but in a way I honestly believe that in some ways I know Daddy better than she does. And the impression I get from him, Hooky, is that he is *scared*. He's afraid of something.'

'Of the affair, if there is one, being found out, you mean?'

The girl shrugged her shoulders.

'I suppose so, yes. But it isn't always as simple as that is it? These cases one reads every day in the papers nowadays. Call girls and all that sort of thing. Suppose Daddy has let one of that sort get hold of him and—oh, you know all the sordid details that get published every now and again. Two way mirrors and whips and things like that. And suppose there are photographs—'

'You think your father may be being blackmailed?'

The girl nodded energetically. 'Yes, I do. Mother thinks so too. I'm sure she does. But she won't admit it. In fact she won't really discuss the thing with me. That's why I've come to you.'

Hooky wished she hadn't. Nobody knew better than he did that every man has got at least one foot of clay; he didn't particularly want to be the means of bringing the fact home to this starry-eyed young idealist. On the other hand she obviously needed help and he wanted to give it to her.

He lit a cigarette and (a trick he was good at) blew a perfect smoke ring that flowed lazily up almost to the ceiling. He watched it thoughtfully until it dissolved into nothing above him.

'Look Janice,' he said at last, 'it sounds quite likely that your father has made a fool of himself over some woman who probably isn't worth a tinker's cuss. A rag bone and hank of hair, but the fool he called her his lady fair. You know how Kipling's doggerel goes. All men do it; always have done it, always will do it. I'm not glorifying it, I'm not defending it, I'm merely saying it as a fact. The great thing is to get it over with and forgotten with the least hurt to everyone. But it's also perfectly possible that your father has got himself into some sort of trouble over money matters. What's he do for a living? What's his business?'

'He's a financial adviser.'

'Is he?' Hooky said, much impressed. 'By God, I wish someone would advise me about my finances. Do you know what my Aunt Theresa says to me, Janice? She says, "The trouble with you Hooky is that you will continue to spend an income you haven't got on things that you don't need." Come to think of it, it's practically a definition of the Welfare State isn't it?'

'I didn't know you had an Aunt, Hooky.'

'My Aunt,' Hooky answered with perverse pride in the matter, 'is not only *an* Aunt, she is the quintessence of Auntism. She's tough, terrifying and tremendous. You must meet her some day.'

'That would be lovely.'

'Don't bank on it. Now, let's get back to your father. What firm does he work for?'

'I don't know.'

'You don't know?'

'It isn't as silly as it sounds really. He used to be with a big legal firm in London. Sir Lucien somebody or other. I can get their address if you want it. But he left them a few years ago because someone else offered him a much better job as financial adviser; well, I suppose finance and law mixed really, the legal side of finances.'

'But you don't know the name of this new firm?'

'No. It's all rather hush-hush. I suppose it's got to do with mergers and take-overs and things like that. Anyway Daddy gets sent off at short notice to various parts of the country, presumably to spy out the land and see how things are going and whether it's worthwhile putting money in, or making a bid for a take-over or whatever. He has always kept entirely dark about it and if that's the way he wants it, OK, that's good enough for me.'

'And has he been away recently on one of these jaunts?'

'Yes. He came home about a month ago. And it's since then that I've noticed all the things I've been telling you about.'

'Where did he go?'

'Neither mother nor I ever knew. He says secrecy is essential in these things and the only way to keep anything secret is not to tell anyone. So he doesn't tell us. And we don't ask. But I do know that this last trip was to somewhere by the sea.'

'How?'

'Because when he's away Daddy rings up twice a week at least to ask how we are getting on at home, and one week-end when he rang and I spoke to him he said something about it being warm enough to bathe.'

Hooky was considerably intrigued by this account; he had long since learnt that there ain't no such animal as an ordinary, humdrum, uninteresting human being. All men (and specially all women) were in some secret corner of their lives extraordinary, un-humdrum, of fascinating interest. He found himself getting caught up in the story of Janice Mellard's father, with its obvious possibilities, its blank passages and its curious silences. 'And in this last month,' he asked, 'since your father came back from wherever it was that he was strolling along the prom prom prom, have you noticed anything unusual, any little detail out of the ordinary?'

The girl thought. 'Well, there was one small thing,' she said at length, 'but I don't suppose it has anything to do with it.'

'Neither do I,' Hooky agreed, but let's hear it nevertheless.'

'It has just struck me—could you bathe at Potter Heigham?'

'God knows. I suppose so. Why?'

'When I'm at home I always get up pretty early; I just like to for one thing, and then I want to see that my old pony's all right and so on. This means that I pick up the post and bring it in. Naturally I sort through the letters to see if there are any for me. I can honestly say that I don't pry into letters for Daddy and Mummy, but of course I'm interested to see whom they are from and whether I recognise the handwriting and so on. Well about two weeks, or ten days, ago there was a letter for my father addressed in writing I didn't know and the post-mark was very clear on it— Potter Heigham. I noticed it because it's a bit of an unusual name and I wondered who it was that Daddy knew there.'

'Did you ask him?'

'No. I didn't. It didn't seem of the slightest importance to me and I just forgot about it.'

'Did your father seem particularly upset after getting this letter?'

The girl thought hard. 'I don't know that he did. No, I can't say that I noticed anything in particular; but he did say he had to go to London the next day, I remember that.'

'Anything else?'

'Two days ago there was a telephone call. I answered it because I was the only one in the cottage at the time. It was a woman's voice asking for Mr. Walker. When I said he wasn't in and was there any message she said, "Just tell him a friend of his rang up will you," and rang off.'

'And did you tell your father?'

'Yes—when Mummy was there.'

'Did he seem upset?'

'He pretended not to be, but actually I think he was, yes. In fact that was what decided me to come and ask you to help.'

A delayed-action fuse went off in Hooky's mind. 'Just a moment,' he said, 'Mr Walker? Is he your father or step-father? I thought your name was Mellard.'

'My stage-name, Hooky. Janice Mellard. That's the name I decided to use on the stage and the name I am one day going to be known by. Really known. At home I'm Janet Walker.'

Hooky laughed. 'Janet or Janice, both nice names,' he said. 'What do you want me to call you?'

'Janice. You're part of my London life, Hooky.'

'OK. Janice it is. And when you talk about "home"—where's that?'

'Magpie Cottage, Rookery Lane, Beaconsfield.'

Hooky nodded, and made a note of the address on a pad.

'Just one final thing,' he warned. 'You do realise, don't you, that when you start digging into anyone's private life you are apt to come across unpleasant things sometimes?'

'Yes, I know that, Hooky. It's because I think there is something unpleasant there that I want you to dig. I want to find out what the unpleasant thing is and put an end to it before it gets any worse.'

'Sensible girl,' Hooky said. 'Leave it to me.'

MOLLY watched the two rashers of bacon under the grill of the electric cooker anxiously. Arthur was rather particular about the way his bacon was done. He liked it grilled not too little, not too much; it had to be just so. Molly watched the grill; kept an eye on the milk so that it didn't boil over; was aware of what the toaster was doing; and had an ear attentive to the progress of the kettle—all these things were done simultaneously and as a matter of instinct; the front of her mind was occupied, as it was all the time nowadays, with other matters—with one other matter...

...how ludicrous, she thought, pulling the pan out from under the grill to see how things were going, that the happiness of three people and their home life could depend on whether a couple of rashers of bacon were properly done or not...yet that was what things were coming to. Arthur was in such a state about something that she was almost beginning to be frightened of him. Yesterday his breakfast bacon had been over-done only a little bit and he had flown into a temper about it—*isn't it worth while taking a little trouble?* and *can't you be bothered to do things as I like them for once?*... She had looked at him steadily and asked,

'What is the matter, Arthur?'

'Nothing's the matter,' he had pushed his cup forward. 'I'll have my coffee, please.'

She poured it for him.

'You keep asking what's the matter,' he said, 'and I keep telling you nothing is.'

'Are you worried about money?'

'Yes if you want to know I am.'

'If it's only that, it's nothing—'

'I don't now what the hell you mean by "nothing". We can't live on *nothing*. Have I ever asked you to do that?'

'I wouldn't mind how little we had Arthur.'

'Wouldn't you? Well, I do mind. I've money owing to me and I'm going to see I get it.' He took a mouthful of coffee and with a sudden burst of irritation demanded, 'And what do you mean by *"if it's only that"*? What's that supposed to mean?'

Molly had turned away to hide the tears that in spite of all her efforts would well up into her eyes...

All men kill the thing they love. Arthur forgot where or when he had first read that terrible sentence, but he knew it was coming true for him. Ever since he had started robbing Mrs Goldblatt—and at first it was almost by accident, the mistake of entering a sum of money in one account rather than another—his one fixed determination had been not to let the world he had somehow allowed himself to stray into to interfere in the slightest way with the world which meant everything to him—his home. With the amazing self-deception of which men's minds are capable the happy owner of Magpie Cottage, Rookery Lane, Beaconsfield, the proud husband of Molly and father of The Piglet, sometimes actually managed to disbelieve in the activities of Captain West and Major Weller, or whatever name he had used in the last coup...*it can't be me doing that, it must be somebody else; well, it isn't the real me anyway* ...

The 'real me' was someone entirely different. And this had been made clear to the man and the woman when he had first agreed to go in with them. His home life was to be something different, apart, sacrosanct.

Now even that arrangement between them had been dishonoured. '...*you wouldn't want telephone calls coming to that cottage of yours in the country asking about that, would you?*' Val had asked him in the South Kensington flat.

'*Don't start telephoning me at home or there'll be trouble.*' It hadn't frightened her in the least; it had only made her laugh. '*You go home and think it over, Arthur.*'

For a week now he had been doing just that. Thinking things over with the result that two human beings who fundamentally loved and needed one another were becoming estranged and desperately unhappy. Molly's thoughts inevitably ran along one course. *If only he would tell me about it, who she is and why he feels he has to go to her*...if only the man she so deeply loved could bring himself to do that, she thought, things would mend; however sordid the truth was she could face it if only he would trust her, and together they could get things right again; if he had squandered money on this other woman, whoever she was, what did it matter? Money was the least part of the problem, they could economise and survive...

But for Arthur Walker money was not a negligible part of his problem. Every coup he had been engaged in with Val and Jimmy had been successful and his agreed 'cut' had brought him in sums varying between a thousand and four thousand pounds. Val had wisely decreed, and Arthur himself had entirely agreed, that the only safe way to continued success was restraint. Greediness would end in disaster. The Bridge-lessons-for-old-ladies approach was a winner. It had proved itself so. But pull it off too often, follow one coup too soon by another one, and you would be ensuring disaster, cutting your own throat; inevitably the law would put together too many agreeing details, would be able to build up a case. Long intervals between, and careful planning had been the strategy so far, and it had proved its worth.

But it meant that the proceeds of each successful coup had to last a considerable time. It invariably happened, therefore, that by the time a fresh haul had been made Arthur was in real need of the money.

As he was now.

He was overdrawn at the bank and very considerably in debt. This state of things was blissfully unknown to Molly who, although not in the least extravagant, regarded her husband as a financial wizard and until his very recent admissions on the subject had never dreamt that he could have worries in that direction.

His share of the proceeds from the Hove affair would have put Arthur's finances on an even keel again and given him something to go on until the next coup. The fact that the ear-marked purchaser of the snuff-boxes had been killed on the main run-way of Ciampino airport was nobody's fault; Arthur realised that. He also realised that something about the money arrangements was nagging in his mind. His thoughts kept going back to the scene in the South Kensington flat '...it isn't everyone in the world who's got fifty thousand pounds to spare' the woman had said. 'I thought it was to be forty thousand,' Arthur himself had interjected.

'It was forty thousand. What did I say? Fifty? Wishful thinking!' But the laugh which had accompanied the explanation had not been convincing and the quick glance between the man and the woman which he had intercepted had disturbed Arthur deeply. There was little enough to go on—a slip of the tongue, an instantaneous eye-message between two people, but for Arthur it had been enough. He was being taken for a ride. He was the mug and they were using him. The accounts were being cooked. Forty thousand as far as he was concerned; fifty thousand for the other two. He would never be able to prove it, but by now, especially after days of brooding over it at home, he felt sure of it.

There was the telephone call.

'Somebody rang you up, Pop, whilst you were out.'

'Oh, who?'

'I don't know. She didn't give her name.'

'She?'

'It was a woman's voice. She just said *tell Mr Walker I rang up, will you?*'

'Oh, I see. Heaven knows who it was. Might be anybody.'

Janet had wanted to make a joke of it; to pull his leg a little; to say something about unknown charmers anxious to get in touch with him. But she realised sadly that she mustn't. Jokes like that belonged to happy, innocent days; and somehow the atmosphere in Magpie Cottage had reached the stage lately when happiness and innocence seemed to be excluded. Besides she had seen her father's face when he had told her airily *'heaven knows who it was'*. Whether heaven knew or not Janet couldn't say; she was quite certain that her father did....

The telephone call had been the deciding point in Arthur Walker's mind.

'Don't you start telephoning me at home or there'll be trouble,' he had told the woman. She had laughed at him and she had telephoned. So there was going to be trouble. He decided that he must go up to London to see her.

It was mid-afternoon; the small living-room was stuffy and the emotional atmosphere in it was sultry and threatened to become explosive. Jimmy had started drinking shortly after eleven o'clock in the morning and had carried on steadily at it ever since. The woman disliked it intensely and despised him for it. With the fatuous persistence of the half-fuddled he had started to complain again about the failure to find a buyer for the stolen snuff-boxes, and although Val knew that it was futile to do so she allowed herself to be drawn into the argument.

'For God's sake, Jimmy, can Benno help it if a pilot coming in to land at Rome pulls the wrong lever, or presses the wrong tit, or something, and lands up in a heap on the run-way?'

'Your precious Benno ought to have somebody else up his sleeve.'

'Benno will find somebody else all right but it takes time.'

Jimmy fished with his hand beside his chair, found the bottle of Teachers and held it up for inspection. 'This bottle's damned near empty,' he said, 'where's it all gone?'

'You ought to know. Down your throat, through your bladder and into the loo. And I don't know what you mean by *my precious Benno*. If I didn't have my contacts for getting rid of the stuff there wouldn't be much point in our picking it up, would there?'

'Then why doesn't he get rid of this lot?' Jimmy mulishly persisted.

The woman shook her head. 'You're not really as stupid as that,' she said; 'you couldn't be. You just make yourself stupid with all the drinking you do. We've had this out a dozen times already, but I'll explain it all again to you in words of one syllable. Some things are easy to get rid of, the market will mop them up as it were without noticing it. But the Arberton collection of snuff-boxes is different. You've got to find somebody who's rich enough to afford them, and who lives far enough away from this country and is powerful enough not to be worried by buying them. People like that don't pop up everywhere. You know all this as well as I do. And I wish to Christ you'd stop sitting there soaking away at that stuff all the time.'

'As soon as this bottle is finished I shall go straight out and buy another one.'

'If you go straight anywhere it will be remarkable after the amount you've put away.'

The man raised his glass.

'Good health to you, and to Benno,' he said.

Val watched him in contemptuous anger.

'You're a damned fool, Jimmy,' she said at length. 'We've been a good team together, but you're spoiling it.'

'If only we could get rid of what we pick up.'

'Oh, not all over again surely—'

The front door bell sounded and the man said, 'You go and see who it is whilst I make quite sure that there's nothing left in this bottle.'

'And supposing it's the law with a search warrant?'

Jimmy, bottle in hand, laughed; he realised that she had asked the question simply to annoy him and that he could score a point by refusing to be annoyed.

'There isn't the slightest chance that it is any such thing,' he replied, 'the snuff-boxes are safe here until you find someone to sell them to. We didn't leave any traces behind. We never do. And the law won't get on to us this time any more than they have before.'

The woman thought he was right; she didn't really think that when she opened the front door she would find someone with a search warrant on the step.

Nor did she. She found Arthur Walker.

She said in a low voice, 'Jimmy's on a jag. He started at eleven o'clock this morning and he's been mopping the stuff up steadily ever since. Do you want to come in?'

'Yes, I do. Never mind Jimmy, he can be as drunk as he likes, I want a few words with you.'

In the living-room Jimmy's ears seemed to have been sharpened in the mysterious way in which semi-drunkenness often works, stupefying one sense, unexpectedly quickening another. 'Come on in, Arthur,' he called out, 'Val's talking a lot of balls, I'm not drunk at all. I'm just drinking.' When Arthur Walker entered the room the man slumped in the chair greeted him genially. 'Have one—if there's any left.'

Arthur shook his head.

'Well, to hell with you then, don't.' In a sudden huff at having his offer refused Jimmy settled himself even more determinedly in his chair and didn't seem disposed to take any more interest in the proceedings. The woman gave him a long contemptuous look and then turned her attention to the newcomer.

'What's your worry, Arthur?' she asked.

'Your telephone call to me at my cottage, that's my worry.'

'Who says I telephoned you?'

'I say so. Janet, my daughter, answered and asked who it was. *Tell him a friend of his called* you said and rang off. What the hell do you think they make of that at home—a woman they don't know, who won't even give her name, ringing up out of the blue and saying that sort of thing?'

'I did warn you, Arthur, I'd be worrying you till you agreed to come in on another job.'

'And I warned you, and I'm warning you again: what I do up here with you two is one thing; my family and home and everything down at Beaconsfield is something else—'

'East is east and west is west and never the twain shall meet,' said the drunken man in the chair.

The woman rounded on him savagely. 'The less you say the better,' she spat out at him. 'If you are going to sit there soaking up whisky all the time the best thing you can do is keep your mouth shut.'

With the elaborate over-caution of his kind Jimmy levered himself up out of his chair and made a more or less steady line across the room. At the door he turned. 'This bloody bottle's empty,' he announced, 'and like I said I'm going out to get another one. You two can go on knocking the hell out of one another as much as you like and good luck to you.'

The two people left behind in the room were silent until they heard the front door slam and for a couple of seconds after. Then the woman turned away and sat, in a sudden gesture of weariness, on the arm of the chair. 'God knows when he'll come back,' she said, 'and when he does you can guess what sort of state he'll be in. Dead drunk. I can't stand much more of it and I'm not going to.'

Arthur Walker looked at her with something approaching compassion. She was such a strong character that it wasn't often he felt sorry for her in any way, but at that moment he did. A little of the angry resolution with which he had left Rookery Lane ebbed out of him. 'Look here, Val,' he said, 'I'm sorry to have come just at this particular moment. I don't like this drinking business any more than you do. Why the hell a man can't see when he's pissed to the wide he's just a nuisance to everybody I don't know. Still that isn't what I came about. I'm telling you fair and square that I'm not having any more phone calls or interference with my private life. It's got to stop.'

And if it doesn't stop, my bold little man, I wonder what the hell you'll be able to do about it the woman thought. But she didn't put the thought into words. As far as Arthur Walker could judge she was taking what he had been brave enough to say to her lying down.

'And there's something else,' he went on, '—the money.'

'Be reasonable, Arthur. I want to get hold of some money just as much as you do; but we can't any of us have our cut till we sell the snuff-boxes.'

'I know we can't. But what I want to be certain of is what we are selling them for—is it forty thousand or fifty thousand?'

The woman was not entirely surprised by the question. She remembered her slip of the tongue; when she had made it she had been aware that it hadn't gone unnoticed by Arthur Walker. She decided that his suspicions would have to be put to good account in forwarding the new plans which were taking shape in her mind.

'That was Jimmy's fault,' she said. 'Of course he was as high as a kite at the time so I don't suppose he really meant it.'

'Meant what?'

'After we had all agreed on asking forty thousand and how it was to be split and you had gone away he said why shouldn't I try to get a bit more and not say anything about it to you.'

'Charming, I must say.'

'I told him it wasn't on, Arthur. The three of us were in it as a team and if I got any more than what we originally talked about we should all have to know about it and share it.'

Arthur Walker looked at her steadily for a few seconds. 'Well, just as long as we are quite clear about that,' he said at last.

'Of course. And anyway Jimmy didn't know what he was saying at the time. He's often like that these days. And you can't run a successful team if one of you is a risk. That's why I don't want him on this next job.'

'What next job? There isn't going to be one for me. I've told you that.'

'You're going straight, is that it?'

'Why shouldn't it be?'

'Because you can't do it, Arthur. And deep down inside yourself, you know that as well as I do. You're bent, and once bent always bent. That's the way the world is. What are you going to do—forget all this and get some job in an office, nine till five every day?'

'Why not?'

'What, give up all the fun of establishing yourself in a new place, with a new personality, getting to know the old ladies and becoming their blue-eyed boy? Give up all that, Arthur? You couldn't do it. You're one of the best con men in the business.'

'What I didn't want was any violence.'

'Of course you didn't. None of us did. At any rate
you and I didn't. Jimmy's a sight too fond of that
bloody knife of his. That's another reason why I don't
want him next time. No violence next time, Arthur.
None at all.'

After a pause Arthur asked, 'And what's Jimmy
going to say to all this?'

'Nothing, because he won't be told.'

'You're just ditching him?'

'He has ditched himself, Arthur. He's drinking
more than ever nowadays and nothing will stop him.
OK, if he wants to be permanently sozzled let him be;
but he's no use to you and me that way, is he?'

Arthur was silent again for a few moments, thinking. Finally he asked, 'How soon can we expect to sell
the Arberton snuff-boxes?'

'Could be quite a time. We might have to wait as
long as a year now.'

'A year? I'll need some money sooner than that, for
God's sake.'

'Of course you will. So shall I. That's what I keep
trying to make you see.'

'So if we did anything without Jimmy what would
it be?'

'The Bridge idea has done us well, wouldn't you
agree?'

Arthur nodded. It had done them well and he was
grateful for it. 'No doubt about that,' he said, 'it's a
first-rate scheme.'

'But it's time to vary it a bit if we don't want to get caught. I think we've worked the South Coast places to death. Especially after what happened at Hove. In all those seaside towns the law will be keener than ever on warning every little Bridge Club they can find to be on the look-out for you. Like I said before, I think we want to shift our ground completely. Go inland. Birmingham, for instance; somewhere like that.'

'And work the same way?'

'Not exactly the same as at Hove. To start with there'll only be two of us.'

'If I come into it at all I'm not doing anything, *anything*, in the way of tying up or gagging or anything of that sort.'

'You won't have to, Arthur. Nobody will. There won't be any of that if we can work my new scheme; and you're so good at your side of things I'm sure we can.'

'What scheme is that, then?'

'You pick your spot and get established as you always do. Group Captain Wilson or Major Wilson, or whatever you are going to call yourself. You look around and find a suitable Bridge Club; there'll be plenty, I'm sure of that. It will be the usual set-up, four or five tables every afternoon mostly of women, some of them well-off, who have nothing better to do.

'Of course I don't have to tell you this part of it; you understand all this and do it marvellously.

'You go through the usual routine of offering to help anyone who wants to improve her game and would like some private coaching. All friendly and for nothing, of course, as per usual. In the end you sort the one old dame who's suitable—lives alone and got something worth lifting.'

'That's the way I've always worked it.'

'So far it is, yes. But we can play the rest of it a bit differently, I think. This time you'll have a car. You can hire one locally when you need it. When you've been giving your old girl a few lessons of private coaching an occasion is bound to come up at the Bridge Club—a tournament or a charity evening, something a bit out of the ordinary—and you tell her you are very anxious for the two of you to play together in it. And what's more you have just acquired a car and will be delighted to call for her and give her a lift. When you call to pick her up and whilst she's in a last minute flap making sure she's got her bag and spectacles and shawl and God knows what, *you* make sure that a downstairs window gets left slightly open. Whilst you and she are winning the tournament at the club I get into the flat, lift whatever it is we have decided on, and away. No violence; nobody hurt; nobody tied up; nothing. When you've finished playing at the club you tell her to wait a couple of minutes whilst you go and get the car from where you parked it and you'll pick her up at the front entrance. And rather naturally that's the last she sees of you. How's that?'

After a long pause Arthur said grudgingly, 'It's neat. I've got to admit that. It's neat. It's got to be thought over for details, of course, but it's workable, yes, it's workable.'

'I can't work it without you, Arthur, it needs the two of us.'

'Well if I decide to come in, it will be fifty-fifty then won't it?'

'All right. Two of us. Fifty-fifty. Even Stephen.'

'*If* I decide to come in, that is.'

The woman's voice hardened perceptibly. 'You'll decide to come in all right, Arthur,' she said. 'You can't really do anything else can you?'

Arthur Walker was riled by her tone and he flushed slightly.

'I'll think it over,' he said rising to leave.

'You do that,' her words followed him out of the door. 'You think it over, Arthur, and let me know. And the sooner the better.'

ELEVEN

DARLING DUGGIE was in his usual position at the far end of the bar. It was early in the evening; the Moon was still uncrowded and none of Duggie's particular circle had yet arrived.

'I'm waiting for some of the silly sods to turn up,' he said, hailing Hooky's advent with evident relief. 'I ought to be bent over my typewriter bashing out fifteen hundred words of brilliant prose about the state of the West End theatre. Jesus, Hefferman, have you had a good look at the West End theatre lately? The Royal Cesspit and the rest of them. Even I can't be brilliant about that lot. And if I can't be, who can? So I'm reduced to coming here and being a sort of human vending machine. The boys put a vodka and lime juice in the slot and out comes a more or less *bon mot*. Rather humiliating really. Eric here thinks it's humiliating. Eric thinks I'm a wasted genius, a total bloody loss; he thinks I ought to do something instead of hanging about waiting for people to buy me a drink. ''Crap or get off the pot'' is Eric's motto, he doesn't believe in inaction do you Eric?'

'I keep what I believe in to myself, Mr Findlayson.'

'*O si sic omnes*. I wish all the bloody religious fanatics in the world would do the same instead of trying to convert one another to the love of a merciful God with hatchets and boiling oil.'

'Was it vodka and lime you said?' Hooky asked.

'And plenty of it,' Duggie answered, pushing his empty glass across the counter. He watched Eric preparing the drink with a critical eye and continued reminiscently, 'My father, may the old fool's bones rest in peace, was a strict teetotaller, which may surprise you—'

'What surprises me, Duggie,' Hooky said genially, 'is to learn that you ever had a father. I've always regarded you as a sort of natural phenomenon, a freak of nature.'

'I was born about three o'clock in the afternoon with a white head and something of a round belly. For my voice I have lost it with hollowing and singing of anthems—not that I expect you to recognise the quotation. Men don't dig for diamonds in the classical mines any more, they spew forth miserable little clay pellets of their own. Put some more vodka into that Eric, Mr Hefferman, although you might not think it, is a generous-minded man. I was about to tell you, before you interrupted me, that my father, who was a strict teetotaller, lived to be ninety-three.'

'That shows how dangerous it is to be a teetotaller,' Hooky pointed out. 'Who the hell wants to stagger on into decrepitude and decay?'

'And do you want to know the old man's recipe for doing the undertakers out of a job?'

'Not in the least.'

'Never marry, never do any work, never stand for Parliament. He used to say that if he hadn't married he'd have got his hundred. What was the name of that girl who bit my ear at the Birleys' party?'

'Her stage name is Janice Mellard.'

'I'm not interested in any other name. As far as I am concerned people who aren't on the stage don't deserve names. They don't exist. Real life? What the laughable hell do you mean by "real life"? There ain't no such thing. Give me the theatre any day for reality. What man makes must be more real than what just happens by accident. Janice Mellard, you're quite right, so it was. For my sins I was watching the box lately and I saw her in something.'

'*Willoughby*.'

'I thought she was good, Hooky. My intellectual honesty and integrity—'

'Your what Duggie?'

'The qualities I have just mentioned compel me to admit that the girl has talent.'

'I'm glad you think so.'

'Presumably you are still interested in her?'

'She intrigues me.'

'You want to see that your flies are buttoned and your cheque book closed.'

Hooky laughed. To take offence at anything Darling Duggie said would have been a tiring business; the man's very existence was virtually one long offence against humanity.

'She's got problems,' Hooky said.

'With you about, plenty. I hope the girl's mother has told her to keep her legs crossed. What sort of problems?'

'She's a client of mine, Duggie. What was it you were so improbably claiming for yourself a moment ago—intellectual honesty and integrity? When it's a matter of my job I, too, am bitten by the same two bugs. What any client of mine tells me comes in at both ears and stays there.'

'In that case,' said Duggie pushing his now empty glass across the counter, 'let us drink to the success of your professional efforts on her behalf.'

'That's a good toast,' Hooky admitted automatically feeling for his wallet...

'Leave it to me,' had been Hooky's cheerful advice to Janice and it wasn't long before he followed it up with some action.

'I'm going to take a trip out to Beaconsfield,' he announced over the telephone, 'to have a look-see for myself.'

He detected the slightest of slight hesitations at the Lammington Gardens end, then the clear young voice answered him, 'Yes, I can see you want to do that, Hooky, and I'd love to ask you to stay for a week-end, but Mummy is inclined to get in a bit of a tizzy over guests; still I'm sure—'

Hooky interrupted her. It wasn't his style to tie himself too closely to his subject. In the early stages of any investigation he always preferred to work from a distance.

'Don't worry,' he answered her. 'I'm not fishing for an invitation. In fact I don't want one. There must be a pub down there I can stay at—'

'There's the Buckinghamshire Arms, I don't know what it's like—'

'Well you'll soon find out,' Hooky said, 'because I'll book myself a room there this Friday and there'll be a nice long cool drink waiting for you at six-thirty or thereabouts. I suggest dinner together afterwards at the pub which will save your Mama any housekeeping worries and incidentally give you and me a chance to have another talk about things; then, after dinner, you can take me round to Magpie Cottage for coffee and to meet your parents—how's that?'

'It's a splendid scheme, Hooky, as long as you don't think it inhospitable of me.'

'It's how I'd like to work things.'

'I'll be there, Hooky. Six-thirty or a little later. Presumably I shall find you in the bar?'

'I should think that's only too likely,' Hooky assured her.... In Gerrard Mews Hooky announced his impending trip to his henchman.

Of all parochial Londoners Roly was the most confirmed; one would imagine that he had been born actually in the belfry of Bow Church.

'Beaconsfield?' He echoed the word as one might say 'Xanadu' or 'Cotopaxi'. 'Where's that, then?'

'In the heart of rural metroland,' Hooky informed him, 'surrounded by swimming pools, deep freezes, two car garages, double glazing, pedestrian precincts and all the other traditional attributes of a sylvan countryside.'

Roly was impressed. 'Blimey, you are going it,' he said. 'And what are you off there for Mr Hefferman?'

'Business, Roly.'

'Business? I should say so. Business with a skirt on, I should think; or most likely with a bikini on the side of one of those double-glazed swimming pools you mentioned. You're a terror, you are, Mr. H. The girls ought to be warned about you. Lock up your daughters. I should say so. And the Mums, too, when you're around.'

'Unlike you Roly I sometimes think of other things.'

'It's a mistake, Mr H. Take my word for it. Concentrate. Remember what the actress said to the bishop: keep your mind on what you're doing and you'll go a lot further...'

Hooky had said nothing definite to Janice about the time at which he intended to arrive in Beaconsfield. And deliberately so. He wanted her to suppose that he would be arriving about six, just in time to establish himself at the Buckinghamshire Arms and await her joining him at six-thirty.

In point of fact he drove his ancient Jag into the hotel car park shortly after three. The mid-day rush was over and there was a pleasant air of somnolence about the place. The attractive young woman on duty at the reception desk seemed pleased to see him. It had added greatly to both the pleasures and difficulties of Hooky's life to date that attractive young women were nearly always pleased to see him.

Hotel receptionists fall into the habit of summing people up pretty swiftly. Watching Hooky approach the counter of her desk this one thought *'hunky, chunky; could be the greatest fun if he liked you, could be a bastard if he didn't. All on his own? I wonder. Not for long anyway, I'll bet....*

'Good afternoon, sir,' she greeted him smilingly. Hooky liked the look of her; business-like, efficient, trim figure, careful hair-do and a weighing-up, slightly mocking look in her eyes; automatically he couldn't help wondering what her afternoon off was....

'...a room, sir?' she said, echoing his request. 'Yes, I think we have. How long will you be staying?'

'Oh, a couple of nights.'

'Just yourself alone, sir?'

'Just myself alone.'

They smiled at one another and Hooky, having decided that the mocking eyes had a greenish tinge in them that he rather liked, added, 'I'm a confirmed bachelor.'

'I was never confirmed myself, my parents didn't believe in it,' the girl with the greenish eyes said, reaching behind her for the key.

When Hooky came out again the car-park attendant was eyeing his Jag admiringly. 'Never mind the new models,' he said as Hooky came up, 'you can't beat the old 'uns as far as I'm concerned. You staying in the hotel, sir?'

'A couple of nights.'

'I'll look after her for you.'

'Good man. How do I get to Rookery Lane?'

'Ah, well, Rookery Lane. That's easy enough to get to, not all that far either. Not in *this* anyway.' He explained the turns and twists which would take Hooky to his goal and then added, 'But you want to be a bit careful, sir. It's a blind road is Rookery Lane. You can't get out at the far end. And if you're going more than half-way down it you'll find turning will be a bit tricky.'

'I shan't be taking the car. I'll be walking.'

'Walking!' The good man's estimation of Hooky clearly fell by several degrees; anybody who possessed the sort of car Hooky had driven down in and then deliberately abandoned it and took to his flat feet was clearly lacking somewhere...

'Well, if you really are walking, sir, of course you won't want to go the way I've just told you at all. Walking, your best way will be up the road to the Old Park, that's just at the end, you can see the entrance gates from here. There's a public pathway through the Park; half-way up the Avenue the path turns off to the left, you'll see it sign-posted, across a field, through a bit of wood and you come out half-way down where you're wanting to be—Rookery Lane.'

'Fine,' said Hooky, 'off I go then. Don't let anyone steal the Jag.'

'I'll watch they don't,' the man answered darkly, regarding Hooky with about as much favour as one would feel towards a callous father abandoning his child.

The callous father set off cheerfully in the mellow afternoon sunshine and the entrance gates of the Old Park showed up in a few minutes, enormous wrought-iron affairs made in a more spacious age. The drive that led away from them curved away grandly under an avenue of splendid limes; whether there was a house or not at the end of about three quarters of a mile Hooky never discovered since after some distance he came across a green and white signpost marked 'Footpath' which pointed across the field on the left just as the Jag-devotee had foretold. There was a stile which Hooky climbed and then sat upon, to light a contemplative cigarette and enjoy the sunny peace of the afternoon.

His enjoyment was marred by the realisation that there was a considerable herd of cattle in the field. When he first seated himself on the stile they had not been visible; then, suddenly, there they were, ranged

round him in a semi-circle, considering him with patient and curious eyes. Unfortunately for him Hooky
didn't realise that the thirty young heifers were merely
patient and curious, bored with being alone in their
pasture all day and anxious for companionship of any
kind. Every man is entitled to one phobia. One man
will lose all reason in an enclosed space; another can't
stand height; the great Lord Kitchener used to be made
physically sick by the mere presence of a cat; Hooky
Hefferman, who by and large was a pretty tough customer and wouldn't admit to being frightened of many
things in life, was scared out of his wits by cattle. At
the back of his mind the small voice of reason kept
trying to assure him that there was nothing to be
scared of; but unfortunately for Hooky the forecourt
of his consciousness was occupied by a totally irra-
tional spectre who kicked the small voice of reason in
the pants and told him if he wanted to feel scared, go
ahead and feel scared. The fact that the young heifers
weren't going to hurt him and that he knew they
weren't going to hurt him had nothing to do with the
case.

Hooky wasn't afraid of being hurt; he was afraid of
the mere presence of this particular sort of animal,
something in their make-up acted on the chemistry of
his own body in a disastrous way. It therefore re-
quired a considerable degree of resolution for him to
toss away his half-smoked cigarette, slip down off the
stile and set out to follow the footpath across the field.

The heifers viewed these proceedings with interest. Since they had been turned into the field shortly after six o'clock that morning they had seen nobody and the advent of a human being was an event for them. They were anxious to know what he was going to do and where he was going. The action of his getting down off the stile made them back away a little; then, as soon as he started on his way across the field, they began to troop after him in an inquisitive manner. Hooky told himself that he mustn't on any account look over his shoulder; but when he had covered about twenty yards he inevitably did so. All thirty heifers were in his wake, the leader of them, an amiable youngster with a black patch over one eye, only a few yards away. Hooky felt a slight sweat breaking out on his forehead . . . *you are the biggest and bloodiest fool in England* he angrily admonished himself, *there is absolutely nothing to be scared of, all you've got to do is continue walking at a steady normal pace till you come to the other side of the field* . . .

After another twenty yards he glanced round again. Black-patch was almost within touching distance. Hooky's heart began to thump a little; *one thing you must not do* he assured himself *is to start to run. That would be fatal* . . .

Within seconds he was legging it over the final thirty yards of the field as fast as he could go. The heifers, delighted by this sudden and unexpected activity, joined actively in the fun and it was almost a photo finish at the far side of the field where Hooky gained the stile giving access to the wood with hardly anything to spare in front of Black-patch. Hooky shot over the stile, thus gaining the sanctuary of a wide grassy ride which led through the wood. It was a minute or two before he recovered his breath and then a voice asked with obvious interest, 'Why were you running away from Farmer West's heifers?' Hooky looked down and saw a small, dark girl, aged (he guessed) about seven or eight. She was carrying a cane rod with a net on the end of it, and an oblong cardboard box. She was an unexpected apparition and for a moment Hooky was at a loss.

'Heifers?' he answered. 'Is that what they are? I thought they were wild bulls.'

'A bull is quite different,' the young wiseacre answered him. 'A bull—'

'All right, all right. None of your practical biology lessons, please. I was only joking.'

'I thought you were scared.'

'Me scared? What of?'

'Of Farmer West's heifers.'

Hooky's dismissing laugh only half disguised the fact that he had already taken an active dislike to this precocious infant.

'I often run like that, just for fun,' he said.

'Do you?'

Hooky thought it was time to carry the war into the Abominable Infant's camp.

'And what are you doing here?' he enquired. 'Ought you to be out in the wood all by yourself?'

'Why not? I'm not scared of anything. I'm catching butterflies. When I catch one I stick a pin through its head and that kills it. It wiggles a bit first and then it dies.'

'Charming, I must say.'

'What are you doing in the wood?'

'I'm making my way to Rookery Lane.'

The Abominable Infant pointed to the grass covered ride. 'If you go along here you'll come to it,' she said. 'And there aren't any heifers or anything like that to be scared of on the way.'

It was becoming increasingly clear to Hooky that child-murder was not such a terrible crime after all.

'Do you know a house called Magpie Cottage in Rookery Lane?' he asked.

'Of course I do. Mrs Walker lives there. My mum works for her.'

'Does she, now?'

'In the mornings. Cleaning. And Miss Walker, Janet, she's been on the telly.'

'Did you see her?'

The Abominable Infant nodded.

'Was she good?'

'Not very. I didn't think so. There wasn't any killing or anything. Are you going to see Miss Walker?'

'M.Y.O.B.,' Hooky said, 'if you know what that means.'

'At school we say it means Mess Your Own Breeches,' the Abominable Infant replied, and Hooky left her; he knew when he was beaten.

The ride led him between ancient and noble oaks for some distance until finally the trees thinned out and lessened in size and Hooky himself emerged at the edge of a steep bank overlooking a narrow country lane.

Rookery Lane, evidently; but which way lay Magpie Cottage? There was no means of knowing and Hooky was on the point of scrambling down the bank to explore when a sound stayed him.

Horse's hooves.

He stopped where he was, in the cover of the ragged hedge that lined the top of the bank, and watched. Within a few seconds a Palomino mare came in sight, dancing a little on her elegant feet and evidently full of beans. Her young mistress was on her back. Janice. Riding in jeans and a trim white blouse that showed off the little hillocks of her breasts to perfection. Bareheaded. She looked, as many girls do, at her best on horseback, doing something she enjoyed doing and doing it extremely well. She was not in the least worried by the Palomino's spirited antics, and together horse and rider sidled away down the lane completely unaware that they were being watched.

Reasoning that a horse as fresh as that must just be starting out Hooky felt safe in determining the direction of Magpie Cottage. Without yet making his way down into the lane he followed the top of the bank until a sudden curve brought his objective in view. There it was, on the other side of the narrow lane; he could actually read the name on the small white gate. It looked a well-cared for homely place. It looked happy. Nothing pretentious about it; the word 'luxury' would never occur to you in connection with it, but the better words 'comfortable' and 'friendly' certainly would. It was the sort of place a man would want to come home to, and studying it from his vantage point behind the hedge Hooky wondered for the umpteenth time in his life on the folly of the human mind.... With a home like this, he speculated, and a daughter like Janice and a wife who no doubt looked after him and loved him why the hell does a man want to go and get tangled up with some little professional hot-pants in London who won't give a second thought to him when his bank balance runs out...

Hooky posed the question to himself not expecting an answer. He knew only too well that there was no answer. The clown is necessary to the circus. In the grand divine concept of the Universe some species had to be cast for the role of Perpetual Bloody Fool. Man had got the part and he played it to perfection.

Hooky sat and watched. He was good at sitting and watching. Many of the most valuable discoveries he had made in his capacity of Private Eye had come to him as a result simply of sitting still and looking.

It wasn't long before his patience was rewarded.

The front door of Magpie Cottage opened and a woman came out carrying a pair of garden clippers and a wooden trug. It could hardly be anyone but Janice's mother. The woman of the house. The everlasting arms which all over the world, in every sort of condition and circumstance, tend, comfort and compassionately hold together the ramshackle and rather shabby world of men.

Putting the wooden trug down by her side she got to work, dead-heading the roses of the front garden. A few minutes later the door of the cottage opened again and Hooky suddenly began to doubt his senses.

He sat bolt upright and leant forward to make what was already a good view even better.

It was an unmistakable view.

There are some things seen so clearly that a man can't believe them even if he wants to. The longer Hooky stared at the scene the more he was convinced. The man now helping in the gardening operations of Magpie Cottage was no stranger to him. Hooky had last seen him at the Bridge table in Aunt Theresa's flat in Wensdale Court, Hove, where he had been the ultra-polite, agreeable Major Weller. Here in Rookery Lane, Beaconsfield, he was Janice Mellard's father.

After watching for long enough to be absolutely certain that he wasn't dreaming or seeing visions Hooky drew back a little from his viewing vantage point, sat on the decaying trunk of a fallen beech tree

at the fringe of the wood and lit a contemplative cigarette. He added things up and they *did* add up, only
too neatly and convincingly. First, there was Janice's
account, trustingly vague and unquestioning, of her
father's business activities: every now and again away
for weeks at a time but without letting his family know
where 'away' was...*employed as financial adviser*.
'Some adviser,' thought Hooky who couldn't help a
certain sneaking admiration for the clever little con
man; then there was the undoubted fact that by accident Pink-Gin-Plummy-Voice of The Raven had, literally, stumbled across the two villains, the man and
the woman, on their way to do the job at Wensdale
Court; and P-G-P-V, though not the town's brightest
citizen, had noticed one thing—the brochure about the
Norfolk Broads in the cubby hole of the car. Add on
to this the letter with the *Potter Heigham* post-mark
idly and uncomprehendingly noticed by Janice and
Hooky realised that virtually without effort on his part
he was well ahead of the professionals.... He also
realised that for once in a way he very definitely
wished that he wasn't ahead of anybody.

'Damn and blast it all,' he exclaimed aloud flicking
away the butt of his cigarette and getting to his feet.

He wished very strongly that Janice Mellard was not
due to dine with him in a few hours' time; he wished
that he had never met the girl....

Shortly after six Hooky approached the reception
desk.

'Still hard at it?' he enquired amiably.

Green-eyes smiled and wondered for an instant whether she was going to be asked what time she came off duty.

'There's always plenty to do,' she temporised.

'I wonder would you do a small job for me—?'

'A votre service,' said Green-eyes who had done the six months' introductory hoteliers' course at the Ecole Domestique in Geneva.

'I'm expecting a young lady to call at about half past six, would you let her know that I am in the small bar, please?'

The agreeable voice of the girl at the reception desk said, 'Of course, Mr Hefferman, with pleasure'; the mocking green eyes of the girl at the reception desk said, quite inaudibly but equally quite plainly, *a young girl calling at six-thirty? I'm not in the least surprised, you chunky piece of masculinity; you haven't wasted much time have you? I wonder what she'll be like, the lucky girl....* 'And we'll be having dinner together,' Hooky continued, 'so could you ring through to the restaurant and ask the head waiter to keep me a table for two?'

'At what time Mr Hefferman?'

'Oh pretty early, say seven-fifteen. We'll be going out after.'

I bet you will, Green-eyes thought. 'I expect you'd like a corner table, Mr Hefferman, would you?' she asked.

'Well, one doesn't want to be in the full glare of publicity does one?'

'I certainly never do,' Green-eyes said. 'Will do, Mr Hefferman.'

The Small Bar, rather heavily overdone with pseudo and sporting prints and other rather less, than more, authentic trophies of the chase was not, at that time, busy. Only two other customers were in it whom Hooky neither knew nor wanted to know. He recognised their type—earnest and serious drinkers on whose devotions he had no desire to intrude. The barman, grave-faced and melancholy with sad eyes, enquired Hooky's pleasure.

Lately in his drinking habits Hooky had strayed down alien paths. Paths pleasant enough in all conscience, but unusual for him. Now, faced with the stress of what he feared must turn out to be an awkward evening, as a child turning to its mother's breast for comfort, he reverted to his first love.

'Can you fix me a Pimm's Number One?' he asked.

'Of course, sir.'

'Then please do so. As large and potent as possible.'

It was a little time later, when Hooky was half-way through the second of the sad barman's excellent concoctions, that Janice came in.

She looked young, fresh, healthy and happy.

She looked like a girl who had recently spent a couple of hours riding her favourite horse in the open air, who had then had a long luxurious hot bath and had afterwards put on a frock which she knew suited her because she was going to have dinner with a man she was beginning to like more than a little. Between first seeing her enter the Small Bar and uttering his opening words of greeting (a matter of one and a half seconds possibly) Hooky was aware of all these things.

. . . God damn it all he thought *what a mess this is*; aloud he sang out cheerily,

'Janice—how nice to see you. What will you have?'

'What's that fascinating looking drink you've got?'

'It's called a Pimm's Number One. A sovereign remedy for indigestion, mental warts, worries, disillusionments, religious convictions and most other ills of the spirit.'

Janice laughed happily. 'I must have one at once,' she said. 'I can't wait to be cured of all those frightful things.'

She was in great form.

When they sat down at the table for two tucked away in a discreet corner of the dining-room she told Hooky why. He was only too glad to let her do all the talking. A time would inevitably come when he would have to say something and he wanted to put it off as long as possible.

'The most marvellous thing happened today, Hooky. This morning. Jimmy Fyson my agent rang me. Agents are pretty good hell as a rule, but still you've got to have one and every now and again they do turn up trumps. Which Jimmy did this morning. I really can't think how he has worked it, or why it should have happened—in fact I can hardly believe it yet—but Jimmy has been talking to Dorset Blagdon who apparently has been watching that T.V. thing I've been in—'

'*Willoughby.*'

'That's the one. And Dorset Blagdon wants me for the lead—the *lead* Hooky, no less—in his new West End production which will go into rehearsal almost immediately and be put on in the autumn. Isn't that wonderful?'

'Local girl makes good, eh?'

'At least local girl has a chance of making good. I'm absolutely terrified, of course.

'Nonsense. You'll do it splendidly. What sort of play is it?'

'I know absolutely nothing about it yet. I'm getting my part, the whole play in fact, to read tomorrow.'

'I wonder if Darling Duggie will like it?'

'Darling Duggie!' Janice rolled her pretty eyes to heaven. 'Oh my God!'

'Perhaps a merciful Providence will arrange for him to be bitten by a poisonous snake before your first night.'

'I wish it would.'

'The trouble is the snake would probably die and not Duggie—still, don't let's worry about him tonight, tell me about Dorset Blagdon; have you worked for him before?'

The great thing from Hooky's point of view was to keep the girl talking for as long as possible and so put off the moment when he would have to tell her (inventing some excuse which he couldn't yet begin to imagine) that he didn't propose to go back to Magpie Cottage after dinner for a friendly cup of coffee with her parents.

And talk away she did, happily and excitedly. And the more she talked the more Hooky realised how difficult things were going to be.

'...*the trouble with you Hooky* (his Aunt not infrequently pointed out) *is that you are always getting yourself into impossible situations...*' He was certainly finding himself in one now. '...one marvellous thing about it,' Janice was explaining, 'is the effect it's already had on Mummy. She's been frightfully down lately with all the stupid business about Father and now my getting a real chance in the West End has bucked her up no end...'

Hooky listened with every sign of enthusiastic interest but inside him a dismal croaking was going on. *What I've got to do* he kept telling himself *is to cut in on all this cheerful-Charley chatter and say: look Janice, your father is a clever con man, one of a gang of crooks who recently robbed my Aunt's flat and in doing so caused the death of an elderly woman and I'm going to the local police to tell them so...*

The more he told himself that this was what he had to do the more he realised that, for the moment at any rate, the shot just wasn't on the board. He simply lacked the moral courage to do it...

Mr Hefferman, please; Mr Hefferman, please. A message for you at the reception desk in the hall. Thank you. The announcement from the loudspeaker of the p.a. system over the dining-room door caused a momentary halt in the general buzz of conversation. As soon as it was ended people started talking again and Janice said, 'That's for you, Hooky. How exciting. What's it all about?'

'I haven't the foggiest.'

'Something from your dubious past catching up with you?'

Hooky looked at her for a moment without speaking, then he pushed his napkin to one side and got up out of his seat. 'That's always liable to happen with anybody,' he said. 'Back again in a minute or two.'

In the hall he was surprised to see the man from the car park in conversation with Green-eyes who was still at her post.

'Sorry to trouble you, sir,' the attendant greeted him, 'but it's this woman who's bashed your Jag. You've never seen anything so stupid. God almighty, I don't know how they give 'em driving licences, I don't really. She drives into my park in this little mini and, "Where can I park?" she asks.

'"Madam," I told her—that's how you 'ave to talk to 'em—*madam*, God's strewth I'd give most of 'em *madam* if I had my way. "Madam," I told her, "there's plenty of room, you can park anywhere you like."

'"Alongside that big car there?" she asks.

'"If you want to," I told her.

'"I think I'll reverse in so it will be easier coming out," she says.

'"Good idea," I said.

'Quite honestly, sir, anyone could have reversed an eight wheel Scammel into the space alongside your Jag; it never occurred to me there was any danger or any possibility of trouble. I wasn't even looking; I had turned away for the moment to pay attention to something else. So the first thing I knew I heard *crash*. I couldn't believe it. This stupid woman had reversed her Mini into the near wing of your Jag. Made a damned great dent in it.

'"What in the name of God did you want to do that for?" I asked her.

'"I'm afraid I must have got on the wrong lock or whatever it's called," she said.

'"*Wrong lock!*" I told her, "people like you ought to be locked up, that's about the truth of it, not go about being a menace to everyone."'

'So where is this lady now?' Hooky asked.

'Standing by the Jag, sir. "You wait there," I told her, "until I get the owner out to get your name and address and all the rest of it. And don't try driving off," I warned her, "because I've got the number of your Mini anyway."'

'And is the damage bad?' Hooky enquired.

'Well, actually it isn't all the bad, sir. Not when you come to examine it. It's the lunacy of it that riles me— all the room in the world and she had to go and do that; in my car park, too.'

Hooky went outside and found an agitated middle-aged woman standing by a little green Mini. He examined the damage to his Jag and wasn't unduly dismayed; the faithful old car had endured worse already in its life and very probably would do so again. He soothed the agitated female. 'Not to worry,' he told her. 'These things happen. We'll just swap names and addresses and who our insurance companies are and so forth as a matter of form. But maybe nothing will come of it.'

The agitated female was much relieved by his reasonable attitude. 'I am most frightfully sorry about it all,' she said, 'I'm afraid I don't really understand about going backwards much.'

Under his breath the faithful car-park attendant relieved his feelings with a long alliterative complicated oath . . .

Hooky, on the contrary, felt no desire to swear. Not often in his life, he realised, would salvation from immediate difficulties come to him in the shape of a middle-aged incompetent woman driver. But it had this time.

He went back into the hotel and halted for a moment by the reception desk. 'Could you get my bill out straight away?' he asked, 'I find I have to go back to London immediately.'

'You won't be staying the night, then, Mr Hefferman?' Green-eyes asked.

'Unfortunately, no.'

I bet the girl finds it unfortunate too, Green-eyes thought, reflecting that whatever way you looked at it men, on the whole, were pretty good bastards...

In the dining-room: 'Hooky—I thought you were lost!'

'Sorry, Janice. And it's bad news I'm afraid. It was a telephone call from London. The police. My flat has been broken into and everything's in a frightful shambles. I've got to get back straight away and see what has been stolen and all the rest of it.'

'You mean you won't be able to come to Magpie Cottage for coffee?'

'I'm afraid not old girl. I told the police I'll get back to Gerrard Mews just as soon as I can.'

'Oh Hooky, I was so hoping—'

'I know, I know, I know. About your father. We'll have to put that off for a bit. A day or two at least till I get this lot sorted out. By the way, you didn't tell your parents my name did you?'

'No. You said not to. You said we would invent something over dinner.'

'Quite right. Your father might know my name as a private investigator and then he would obviously be suspicious. So keep it back still. Just go on thinking about your own good luck in getting a leading part—'

'Quite honestly I'm finding it hard to think about anything else at the moment.'

'Why should you? Let everything else ride for a bit. I'll be in touch later and we'll see what happens.'

Hooky drove his now slightly dented Jag back towards London slowly. He was doing a lot of thinking. But fast though his thoughts buzzed round and round they didn't get him anywhere much. All the time he could hear echoing at the back of his mind words of wisdom from the Oracle at Hove...*the trouble with you, Hooky, is that you are so apt to think you can solve a difficulty just by putting it off*... True, O Queen, he thought, true; but putting off the evil day was all he could do at the present. What came next he just didn't know...

TWELVE

'ARTHUR don't you think it would be nice if we all had a small glass of brandy with our coffee when Janet and her boy friend come in?'

Arthur Walker was in fact a very temperate person but he agreed heavily with this suggestion.

'Good idea,' he said, 'I'll get it out.'

'I wonder what he'll be like?'

'Now don't start dreaming dreams, old lady. Janet must know plenty of men up in London; it just happens that this one is spending the week-end in Beaconsfield so naturally they are seeing one another.'

'You're like all men, Arthur, miserably unromantic. Having dinner together at the Buckinghamshire Arms—'

'That was to save you the trouble of extra cooking. Janet has always said if one of her boy friends wants to have the fun of taking her out the least he can do is buy her a good dinner.'

'You make it all sound so horribly commercial.'

'Sound commonsense I'd say. I don't think modern girls are commercial particularly; I think they are just level-headed about things.'

'And wanting to bring him back here for coffee—'

'That's just a friendly gesture to show that she doesn't mind us being in on the act and that everything's above board.'

'Anyway there's plenty of cause to celebrate about the part she has just been given in this new play. That really is wonderful for the girl. I know you think I'm just an adoring mum, Arthur; but quite apart from that I think that that girl of ours has got talent. This is just the sort of start she has been praying for and if nothing comes along to spoil her career I think she might make a really big name for herself.'

Arthur heard; but he didn't make any comment; he busied himself getting out the brandy and the brandy glasses. But when Janet appeared she was alone.

'Janet, where's your friend?' Molly demanded.

'Speeding up the A40 at the moment.'

The girl watched the look of consternation spread over her mother's face and burst out laughing.

'I'm awfully sorry to disappoint you Mummy,' she said, 'but this isn't a lovers' quarrel: *a* we aren't lovers and *b* we haven't quarrelled. Just as we were finishing dinner a telephone message came from the police to say that his flat had been broken into and they wanted him to go back straight away to say what has been stolen and see to all the formalities. So off he went.'

'Good heavens, a burglary! It's simply awful the way they are happening all the time. Will he be down here again?'

'I expect so. Do I spy brandy glasses?'

'We thought we ought to celebrate your good news.'

'I'm all for it. I feel on top of the world. Come on, Pop, pour it out.'

His wife and daughter went to bed early that evening but Arthur stayed on half watching, half not caring about, a programme on television. Presently he got tired of the rather aimless talk and turned the set off. Switching out the lights he settled down comfortably in front of the electric fire with his thoughts.

He had plenty to think about.

The evening had been a happy one. Janet was naturally in the highest of spirits, and because the girl was so elated her mother had been excited too, so that for once the irritations and annoyances between Arthur and his wife which had been all too frequent lately had been forgotten. 'If a man can be happy at home,' Arthur thought staring at the single red bar of the fire, 'he can't really ask for much more . . .'

He wondered once again how the hell he had ever been fool enough to start on the path which had led him into the mess that now engulfed him.

A mess which threatened to get worse rather than better. Now, if he wasn't careful, he was going to find himself tied up more than ever with the woman; with Jimmy the lush left out of it.

Left out of it; and almost certainly hostile as a result. Arthur didn't fancy the idea of making an enemy of Jimmy and that knife of his.

'I wish to God I was shot of the pair of them,' he told himself...

Of course, thinking over the plan which Val had just put forward he had to admit that it had its points. Just the two of them; the preliminary confidence work; then no violence, not even any tying up or gagging this time; and a fifty-fifty share-out at the end. It sounded all right; but you never knew with Val; or, rather, you *did* know only too well; you knew that she would never be content with just this one job in the Midlands she was talking about; there would be another one after it and another after that and in the end something would go wrong somewhere and she wouldn't hesitate to use violence to try to get herself out of it... And he would have to tag along and behave himself and do what he was told—or else...

That was what Arthur Walker didn't like. He knew quite well that he wasn't the strongest character in the world, but he didn't like the woman cracking the whip over him... to hell with her, he thought: *once bent always bent* she had said; but why, why, why did it have to be so? *'You'll decide to come in Arthur,'* she had told him, *'you can't really do anything else can you?'*...

He thought back to the happy evening behind him and to what Molly had said about their daughter: *if nothing else comes along to spoil her career*... All too possible headlines and scraps of conversation formed in his head:

'Father of West End Star jailed for theft.'

'...I wasn't likely to get the part, Daddy, was I, with you having just been sent to prison?'...

Ultimately he turned off the fire and making his way out of the room in the dark went upstairs to bed a worried and unhappy man...

The next morning at breakfast there was a letter for him. He waited until he was safely away from his womenfolk before opening it. It was headed with the address of a hotel in Edgbaston, Birmingham, and Val wrote: '...I have been having a preliminary look round up here and I am quite sure we can very soon get on to a good thing. In fact I have one specific thing in mind I want to talk over with you. I shall be back in London on Thursday. Jimmy won't be there because he has been staying with his sister whilst I've been away and doesn't return till Friday. So Thursday afternoon, please. Three o'clock. I can tell you all I've found out and we can talk the whole thing over and lay plans. Don't be later than three...'

On Thursday morning Arthur announced,

'I've got to go up to London today, Molly. Business.'

'Oh dear, does that mean you'll be away for three or four weeks again on one of those jobs of yours?'

'Why should it mean that?'

'I'm only asking, Arthur. I naturally want to know. Will you be coming back tonight?'

'Of course I shall be coming back tonight; why the hell shouldn't I be?'

'I just wanted to know, Arthur, that was all.'

Just before a quarter to three Arthur rang the bell of the house in South Kensington and was surprised when the door was opened by Jimmy. Surprised and slightly dismayed; and although Jimmy was already rather more than half drunk he was still perfectly capable of recognising those two emotions in the face of the man standing on his doorstep. He wondered what the hell Arthur had showed up for, out of the blue...

'Come in, Arthur,' he said. 'What brings you here?'

'I was in London for the day; I thought I'd look in and see how things are going.'

The two men went from the tiny hall into the living-room and Jimmy settled down in his chair and automatically reached for his glass.

'Expecting to see Val were you?' he queried.

'Not especially. Both of you.'

'Well, you're lucky to see either of us. I oughtn't to be here really. Not till tomorrow. I went for three days down to my sister in Sydenham whilst Val's away. Or didn't you know she was away?'

'How should I?'

Jimmy laughed. 'Have a drink, Arthur?'

'No thanks—'

'For Christ's sake don't go and say it's too early for you. I know it's early. But as far as I'm concerned it's never too early for a drop of Scotch. You and Val are a pair together with this psalm-singing, TT business.'

'You drink all you want to, Jimmy.'

'Don't bother, I shall. No bloody woman is going to dictate to me what I do, I can tell you that.' He filled up his glass from the bottle of whisky and went on, 'So you just looked in to see us on the off-chance eh?'

'That's it.'

'Well, everything's all right, Arthur. The Law hasn't been round asking about Hove. And it won't be, don't bother. Only about forty-eight per cent of jobs get rumbled by the Law; and ours belong to the fifty-two per cent that don't.'

'Only we haven't sold the snuff-boxes yet.'

'Too bloody true, Arthur; we haven't sold the snuff-boxes yet.'

The shrillness of the telephone interrupted them and Jimmy reached out a hand to deal with it. After the first few seconds it was clear who was ringing up and Arthur listened to Jimmy's half of the conversation with some private amusement.

'...of course it's me, who did you expect it to be?...I *did* go down there...and that's right, I *was* staying till tomorrow; but I changed my mind, is there any law against that?...all right, all right...I came back a day early because my sister's as bad as any of you women, nagging at me all the time about how much I drink...all right, all right, I *do* realise it, don't you start over the phone for Christ's sake. What are you ringing up about, anyway?...a one day strike? It's time some of those bastards stopped talking about strikes and did an honest day's work for a change... well, you'll have to stay till tomorrow won't you? Arthur's here...how should I know what he wants? He's in London for the day so he looked in to see us. Nice of him wasn't it?... Tomorrow, yes, all right, all right, tomorrow...'

He replaced the instrument and reached for his glass again. A thought was buzzing before he realised what it was...

'So that was Val was it?' Arthur enquired.

'Um. Natter, natter, natter.'

'What was all that about a one-day strike?'

'It seems the railway types at Birmingham have got a dispute on suddenly and there won't be any trains till tomorrow.'

'There's always something.'

Jimmy's troublesome thought had suddenly clarified itself, and he looked across at Arthur.

'Val thought I was with my sister down at Sydenham,' he said. 'As far as she was concerned I *was* down at Sydenham—*so what was the point of ringing up here?*'

The two men looked at one another and Arthur hoped that his face wasn't betraying anything. He felt a little scared all of a sudden.

'I suppose she made a mistake.'

Jimmy shook his head.

'Val doesn't make mistakes like that. Besides when I answered the phone she said *I thought you would be with your sister*—so who did she think would be here?'

'I suppose she rang up on the off-chance that you might have come back.'

Jimmy poured some more whisky into his glass and tossed it down in one gulp.

'Do you, Arthur?' he asked, 'do you?'

A few seconds later Jimmy spoke again. 'It's a bit funny, isn't it, Arthur, that you should just happen to call here this afternoon and Val should just happen to ring up at the same time? Just happen. Is there anything going on between you two?'

Arthur Walker's heart missed a beat or two. 'Don't be silly, Jimmy,' he answered as convincingly as he could. 'What do you mean by that?—"*anything going on*"? Of course there isn't.'

Jimmy held up the whisky bottle for inspection and seemed satisfied by what he saw in it.

'Of course I'm only a bloody fool. I know that,' he said. 'I'm there for the rough stuff. Not your line at all, Arthur. You think the world goes round without any rough stuff. Gentle Jesus meek and mild. You're clever. Oh, I'll give you that. You're a good con man, Arthur; you're a very good con man. We couldn't turn the trick without you. Mind you, it would do you all the good in the world to go out and get as pissed as a newt every now and again and poke the hell out of some fat tart in Jermyn Street; but that's not your style is it, Arthur? And I don't mind telling you one thing, Arthur'—having emptied his glass by generous sips as he was talking Jimmy now filled it again. 'I don't mind telling you one thing—I like you. Always have done. So I don't want to see you being made a bloody fool of.'

'What do you mean by that Jimmy?'

'If Val's inviting you to get up to any tricks just you be careful, Arthur. She'll take you for a ride. She'll twist the balls off you. I suppose you thought you were getting a square deal over the money for the snuff-boxes didn't you? That woman wouldn't give a square deal to her dying father.'

Arthur pondered for some seconds before answering all this; finally he made up his mind and said quietly, 'She told me it was you who wanted to do me out of some of my cut.'

'Ah, did she?'

'She said I was to be given a cut on the price we first talked about which was forty thousand, but that she would really be getting fifty thousand and you two were going to split the extra up between you.'

'Christ, I'll trim her for telling you that,' Jimmy said. 'Wait till I get that bitch down here tomorrow, I'll read her a lesson.'

'It's no good us all falling out over it, Jimmy.'

'Why don't you join the Salvation bloody Army and go round with an effing tambourine preaching to everybody? What did you come here this afternoon for, anyway? She'd have been here, too, if it hadn't been for that strike. I suppose you two were going to talk over something together and leave me out of it?'

'Of course not, Jimmy.'

'Of course not, Arthur!'

The two men looked at one another and the thought uppermost in Arthur Walker's mind was an intense desire not only to leave Jimmy out of everything but the woman as well, to free himself of both these people.'

'Do you know what I'm going to do now?' Jimmy asked, 'I'm going to finish this bottle. Then I'm going to have a nice bit of shut-eye till half past seven or eight this evening and when I wake up I'll go out on the town on a real bender. I want to be in proper form to deal with that slippery partner of mine when she shows up tomorrow.'

'In that case I think I'll be going.'

'You do that, Arthur. You toddle off back to Beaconsfield or wherever it is.'

'Incidentally she's my partner as well, you know.'

'If I find she's been up to any tricks she won't be in a fit state to be anybody's partner for a bit, I can promise you that.'

Arthur Walker pulled the living-room door to behind him and stood a moment in the narrow hall. His thoughts were racing ... God Almighty, what a jungle to have got myself into, what a jungle ... *if nothing comes along to spoil her career ... you're a good*

con man, Arthur, a very good con man ... just be
careful Arthur she'll take you for a ride ... and then
that drunken fool in there giving me advice ... *get*
pissed as a newt ... I wish to God I was out of this lot
altogether, shot of the pair of them ... *I feel on top of*
the world, come on Pop, pour it out ...

In the hall there was a small table; on it, an electric
torch, a pair of gloves and a key ring with a single key.
In the course of persuading trusting old ladies and not
so trusting landladies that he was someone other than
he really was Arthur had often had to make quick de-
cisions.

He made one now.

He picked up the key ring with its single key and
slipped it in his pocket.

Ten seconds later he had closed the front door of the
flat behind him and was walking in the direction of
South Ken station. But South Ken station, although he
would be using it eventually, was not his immediate
destination. Walking slowly and thinking furiously he
went beyond it and carried on until he found a friendly
looking tea-shop. On his way he bought an *Evening*
Standard but he had finished his tea and a contemplative cigarette as well before he bothered to open the
paper. When he did what caught his eye was not the
front page with its usual screaming announcements of
disaster but a paragraph in the Gossip Column.

'Dorset Blagdon, the controversial young producer, has come up with what he assures me will be a

real winning double. He has discovered a new playwright ("of genius" Blagdon says) and a young actress who he is confident will be the new star of the West End theatre. Anthony Ledborough is the playwright and his play *The Burnt-Out World* which Dorset Blagdon is to produce in the autumn will star Janice Mellard in the leading part. If you have noticed *Willoughby* on T.V. recently you will have seen Janice, but Dorset Blagdon says he hopes you didn't. That was only a trial run he says, "if she doesn't fall down and break her neck or anything silly like that Janice Mellard is booked for stardom."'

Arthur Walker read this paragraph twice and then skimmed through the rest of the paper. At a quarter past four, when his waitress was obviously becoming a little impatient, he stubbed out the cigarette he was smoking and asked for his bill.

'Everything all right?' the girl asked.

'Yes thanks,' Arthur told her. 'Everything's OK now.'

It was something after twenty past when he stood outside the front door of the flat again. He hesitated slightly, but only slightly; then he rang the bell. He had his excuse ready if Jimmy should come to the door...*sorry Jimmy to trouble you, I've lost my glasses, did I leave them here by any chance* ... but he didn't think he would have to use it; he didn't think anybody would come to the door; he thought that Jimmy would be doing exactly what he said he would be doing—sleeping off the effects of a day of pretty well continuous drinking.

There was no answer to the bell. Arthur waited a few moments, then to make sure, rang again. Still no answer. Now he waited no longer. Very quietly he put the key in the Yale lock, very quietly opened the door and went inside. For a moment he stood just inside the hall apprehensive, listening. Then his ears were gratified by one of the most unmelodious but at the same time unmistakable sounds in the world—a man snoring. A regular rhythmical harsh intake and expulsion of breath coming from the living-room. Arthur Walker gently pushed the living-room door open and saw what he expected to see: the man Jimmy stretched out on the sofa, his face flushed, an empty glass on the floor beside him, in a heavy drunken sleep. A troupe of marauding monkeys exploring the room wouldn't have woken the man and Arthur Walker could move much more quietly than any monkey.

He pulled the door of the living-room to and took five steps to the cupboard under the stairs. Very carefully he moved the Hoover to one side and the two suitcases stacked beyond it. Behind the suitcases hidden by an old piece of carpet was a dark blue travelling bag. He didn't even bother to undo the zip to see what was inside; he knew what was inside.

He replaced the piece of carpet, the two suitcases and the Hoover, and then, for a moment stood, bag in hand, listening. There was no alteration in the rhythm and regularity of the snores coming from the living-room. Arthur Walker put the key back in its place on the hall table and with infinite caution let himself out into the street and pulled the door to behind him. Then quickening his steps he mingled in the early evening crowds making their way to South Kensington station, carrying the dark blue bag.

THIRTEEN

VAL SETTLED DOWN in a corner seat of a first-class smoking compartment in New Street station, Birmingham. She had had words with the ticket inspector at the entrance to the platform.

'Nice of you to let us use our railways again,' she had said.

'Yesterday's little bother was nothing to do with me, madam.'

'No, of course not. It never is to do with anybody, is it? Always somebody else; but the public get kicked around just the same, don't they?'

'Your train is the Inter-City standing there on the left, madam.'

The Inter-City was not crowded and only two other passengers got into Val's compartment, both men. She was aware that the younger of them was viewing the length of leg she was displaying with interest. She would have been disappointed if he hadn't shown interest. By now she had learnt that she was not what people called 'pretty' and had become reconciled to the fact; but she was tall with long, well-shaped legs and the indefinable, provocative elemental thing emanated from her; almost without troubling to do so she looked sexy. In a way this was odd because sex with her and Jimmy had ceased to have any attraction for her; had, in fact, almost ceased to exist.

She drew on her cigarette and thought about Jimmy. Jimmy had been a good partner once and she had done well with him; but he had become a risk and a liability, and whether Arthur agreed to come along or not the only sensible thing was to shed Jimmy and start afresh. Of course she would have to put up with him until the Arberton snuff-boxes were sold. She realised that. Or at any rate, she amended in thought, he would have to get his cut of the proceeds when the snuff-boxes were sold. Otherwise he would turn nasty. And Jimmy, as she well knew, was capable of turning very nasty indeed.

Jimmy would have to be handled carefully, but she was confident she could manage that; the occasional interested glances which the young man opposite shot round the edge of his *Daily Telegraph* increased her confidence; one way or another, fly-buttons or bottle, men were pretty easy meat....

She turned her thoughts to Arthur. A good con man, no denying that. A natural. And in spite of the slight noises of dissent he had been making he was obviously going to come in on the Edgbaston job. Whether she would want to go on working with him after that she herself wasn't certain; but if she did want him—a grim little smile played across her face for a moment—if she did want him Arthur would come to heel when she twitched the rope....

A taxi took her from Euston to South Kensington. She paid the man off and let herself into the house. Jimmy would be sloshed, of course; she expected that; and for once in a way she hoped it would be so; she realised that in all probability there would be difficulty over her unfortunate telephone call of the previous afternoon and she reasoned that Jimmy would be easier to deal with sufficiently fuddled by Scotch than otherwise. Whilst she was still in the hall Jimmy called from the living-room.

'That you?'

His voice didn't sound drunk; nor, somehow, did it sound quite normal. She was puzzled by it, and put on her guard, even slightly afraid. She opened the door of the living-room and went in. Jimmy was sitting in his customary chair, with his customary reading matter (the racing edition of the *Evening Standard*) in his hand, but without the customary glass anywhere in sight.

'Aren't you having a drink?' she asked.

'Why should I if I don't want to?'

'Well, I think I'll have one.'

'You do that.'

He watched her as she crossed to the corner cupboard where the bottles and glasses were kept. She was aware of his eyes on her all the time and she didn't like it. There was something odd about the whole situation. She turned, drink in hand, and felt that she had to say something.

So she said, 'How I hate trains.'

'You must have come Inter-City.'

'Yes, I did.'

'I'm told they are very comfortable.'

'I suppose they are all right. I just dislike trains, that's all.'

He had nothing to say to this, and since she found the silence that intervened uncomfortable she broke it.

'And how did you get on at your sister's?' she asked.

'She got on my wick with her everlasting snide remarks about how much I was drinking. Like I told you. When you rang up.'

'Poor Jimmy!'

'When you rang up.'

... This is it, she thought; there's danger here and I'd much sooner have him half sloshed than stone cold sober which amazingly is what he appears to be....

'Why shouldn't I ring up? Any law against it?' she enquired lightly.

'What was the point of ringing up when as far as you knew I'd still be down at Sydenham?'

'I forgot which day you said you'd be coming back, Jimmy.'

'You bloody liar.'

'Have a drink, Jimmy, and cheer yourself up. You're letting yourself get upset.'

'Upset? Christ, that's rich, that is. And why did Arthur Walker call here yesterday afternoon just when, if it hadn't been for the strike, you would have been here as well?'

'I suppose he thought he would look in on spec.'

'That's what you suppose it is?'

'Jimmy, have a drink like I said and cheer up for God's sake.'

'I'll have a drink when I want one. In a minute or two. Don't worry. You and Arthur are up to something, aren't you?'

Val seated herself on the arm of a chair and crossed her legs, hitching her skirt up high. Her length of shapely leg had had an effect on the young man opposite her in the train; in spite of all the indifference that had grown up between them it might still have some effect on Jimmy.

'Let's talk sensibly, Jimmy,' she said in a friendly tone.

'All right then. You talk sensibly. Go on, go ahead. What about?'

She knew she wasn't getting through to him but she persevered. 'You and me, I mean. We've been a good team. We've done well.'

'So what?'

'There's a time for everything, Jimmy. The Bridge lark I thought up has done us proud; but we've used it up. Anyone who goes on long enough with the same game gets caught in the end. Bound to. The Law gets wise to how you work the thing and they warn people in advance and if you go on too long you get caught.

You know that just as well as I do. We've got to be a
bit smarter than that, Jimmy.'

'You fancy yourself at being smart don't you?'

'Never mind about that. It's like I said, there's a
right time for everything and it's time for you and me
to split up. The Law won't know we've split up, they'll
be looking for us together, working the same old
game; and we shall be separated, doing different
things and getting away with them.'

'You're telling me you're tired of me, is that it?'

'I'm telling you to be your age. Christ, Jimmy, we
aren't two romantic kids in a sob stuff movie.'

The man walked over to the table where the drinks
were and poured himself out a large measure of
Scotch. He took a mouthful of the neat whisky, rolled
it round his palate and made a grimace as he swallowed it and the fiery taste of it bit him. He faced her
and said, 'You never did go much for what you call the
romantic line did you?'

'I told you, we aren't two kids in a movie. And
anyway if I'd enjoyed what I was getting it might have
been different. You aren't much good at it are you,
Jimmy?'

The man's face flushed with anger.

'You bitch,' he said quietly.

'Ah, what's the point in calling one another names
and quarrelling? We're washed up, Jimmy. You know
that. You go your way and I'll go mine.'

'Yeah. It isn't as simple as that though, is it?'

'What do you mean?'

Jimmy took another swig at his drink before saying, 'What I mean is, I don't like being twisted over money, not by anybody.'

The woman didn't like the way the talk was going and she didn't like the oddness of Jimmy's attitude. Making her voice as light as she could she answered, 'What's that supposed to mean? Nobody likes being twisted, if it comes to that. What money anyway?'

Jimmy shot out a hand and grasped her shoulder. The harshness of his grip made her wince and she thought if this bastard starts any rough stuff I'll clobber him. But she began to be scared . . .

'You and I used to be partners,' Jimmy said. 'Used to be. Remember? Before you got tired of what I could give you in bed and started showing me that you didn't think I was any good at it. Like you told me a moment ago—'

'I didn't mean that, Jimmy.'

'No? But you said it, you bitch, didn't you? And Arthur Walker wasn't really in the partnership. Not like we two were. We called him in to do the preliminary con man stuff and we two finished off and cleared up. So if we wanted to fix a bit extra between ourselves and not say anything to him about it, why shouldn't we? *As long as neither of us said anything to him about it. . . .*'

The woman said nothing because for the moment she didn't know what to say. The pressure of the man's grip on her shoulder increased and hurt her.

'But one of us did say something,' he went on. 'You did. You told Arthur I had suggested we got a better price than forty thousand and split the difference and told him sweet f.a. about it.'

'You don't believe I told Arthur that, Jimmy, do you?'

'Yes, I do.'

'That's just Arthur's talk.'

'Is it? I wonder. I believe there's something up between you two. Are you getting something from him that you tell me I'm no good at?'

'What! Arthur? Don't be silly. He wouldn't look at any other woman than that little wife of his tucked away in their country cottage. He wouldn't know what to do if he got into bed with me.'

'Wouldn't he? But he knew enough to be here yesterday afternoon in time to meet you if you hadn't been delayed by that nonsense on the railway, didn't he?'

He released his grip on her shoulder at last, turned away and poured himself out another drink.

'After Arthur left yesterday I got stoned,' he said, 'absolutely stoned out of my mind.'

'You do surprise me.'

He faced her again. 'Anyway,' he went on, 'how did you get on up in Birmingham, then? Did you find the fresh contact you were hoping to for getting rid of the snuff-boxes?'

'No. I didn't.'

'But that's what you told me you were going up there for, wasn't it?'

'That's what I told you, Jimmy; but I couldn't pull it off. The man who was going to put me in touch with the Frenchman who might ultimately turn out to be a buyer couldn't get hold of him. So it was no go. Two Inter-City journeys for nothing.'

Jimmy stared at her in silence for a few seconds. Drink was beginning to sharpen his imagination, and a suspicion suddenly assailed him out of the blue.

'Was that what you really went up there for?' he asked at last.

'Of course it was. What else?'

'You didn't take the snuff-boxes up there with you by any chance did you?'

'For God's sake what would I do that for?'

The suspicion was attacking his mind like a poisonous toadstool.

'I'll tell you what you would do that for,' he said. 'I'll tell you exactly what you would do it for. You're tired of me. You've said so yourself. I'm a lush and you don't like the way I fuck you any more. You've got little Arthur in tow now. You heard of a chance up in Birmingham of getting rid of the snuff-boxes at a cut price; maybe half what we were originally hoping for. Never mind, that wouldn't be a bad little sum for you and Arthur to share between you. No third party. No me. I'm out. So you take the boxes up to Birmingham, sell them and then you and Arthur, just the two of you, are off together somewhere.'

'You're out of your mind. I'm leaving till you come to your senses.'

He took a quick stride forward, seized her right wrist and doubled her arm up behind her back so that the pain was intense.

'Christ, Jimmy—'

'Christ away as much as you like. You're not leaving this flat till we've had a look under the stairs together.'

Still keeping her arm doubled up behind her he forced the woman out of the living-room into the hall and to the curtained opening of the stair-cupboard. There he pushed her forward so that she half stumbled and landed on her knees.

'All right,' he said, 'you fetch the bag out with the snuff-boxes in it—if it's still there.'

She was thoroughly frightened now, but there was nothing to do but fall in with his stupid obsession; nor, as she was certain, anything to lose by it. The cupboard under the stairs was dark but not totally so. He could make out what she was doing and in any case she knew what was there. Everything was as it should be: the Hoover which she manoeuvred to one side, then two suitcases which she lifted out of the way and finally the old bit of carpet. . . .

When she moved the piece of carpet she froze for a moment with astonishment. *The dark blue travelling bag was not there....* Astonishment was superseded by fear. Something, she was not sure what, had gone desperately wrong and she was in danger....

'Fetch the bag out then and let's have a look at it,' Jimmy urged from behind her.

She turned round, straightened up and faced him. He stared at her, sure now of what she was going to say. She was frightened to say it; but there was nothing else to do. She said it.

'It isn't there.'

He nodded his head slowly. He was quite certain now that all his suspicions were right. He felt a pulse beginning to hammer in the side of his neck.

'Well, that is a surprise, isn't it?' he said quietly. 'God Almighty, so that's the game is it?'

She saw his hand begin to move towards his inside pocket and she knew what he kept there.

'I'll mark you,' he suddenly snarled. 'Christ, I'll mark you.'

The woman didn't hesitate. Fear made her act. She knew what he was capable of doing with that knife of his. She sprang at him pushing him violently in the chest; the suddenness of it took him off his guard; he lost his balance for a moment and was sent backwards, hitting his head hard against the wall behind him. When he had recovered the woman was already at the front door fumbling at the catch to get out.

FOURTEEN

ARTHUR WALKER had spent most of the day by himself. Janet had left the cottage directly after breakfast, riding her Palomino over to High Wycombe where the mare was entered in one of the classes of the annual County Horse Show. Molly had followed in the car an hour later and the two of them were making a whole day's outing of it, taking a picnic meal and telling Arthur to expect them when he saw them.

'Why don't you come too, Pop?' Janet suggested, but her father shook his head; horsy events weren't much in his line and he was quite happy to be on his own in the cottage.

'There's pork pie and salad and cheese, all in the fridge,' Molly told him.

'I shan't starve then, shall I?'

'And there's fruit if you want it.'

'Lovely.'

'And you can make yourself a cup of coffee if you feel like it. And you'll be all right for tea won't you?'

'Stop fussing, old girl, for heaven's sake. Of course I shall be all right.'

Molly smiled, but didn't look entirely convinced. In her experience men wanted a lot of looking after; and usually the nicer they were the more looking after they needed.

'Go off and enjoy yourself,' Arthur told her. 'Don't worry about me, I'll find plenty to do.'

Much as his whole domestic life depended on Molly he found it rather fun to have the cottage entirely to himself for a day. He spent the morning trimming back the badly overgrown hedge at the bottom of the garden. It was arduous work and he welcomed it largely because it was arduous, and he could concentrate on it and not worry too much about his thoughts. But however hard he tried to occupy his mind with hedge clipping he could not stop his thoughts returning every now and again to other matters. What he had done in South Kensington had seemed to him at the time to be a brilliant stroke; he had visualised it as putting him in a position of power, but on reflection he was more inclined to think that all he had done by it was to put himself in a position of danger....

As he worked away at the overgrown and straggling hedge the bitter, useless, regret echoed again and again through his head: *I wish to God I had never started it; once bent she said to me always bent and it's true; you want to escape, but you can't....*

At lunch time he opened the fridge and there, arranged as neatly as she always did everything, was what Molly had promised: a small pork pie (of which Arthur was very fond), an appetising looking plate of salad and the cream cheese. He opened a bottle of beer and sat in his shirt sleeves in his kitchen—a man taking his ease in his own domain. He was able to put the thoughts that had been troubling him during the morning out of his head at least for the time being. He felt happy.

He didn't bother about the cup of coffee that Molly had suggested but sat reading the paper for a short time after he had finished eating; then he was out in the afternoon sunshine again. Sweeping up the hedge trimmings was almost as big a job as clipping it had been, and when he had finished that he raked out a mass of dead leaves and rubbish that had been allowed to accumulate behind the garden shed.

Hedge trimmings, dead leaves and rubbish were all taken in a succession of barrow journeys to the bonfire site; paper and matches were brought out from the kitchen and Arthur Walker busied himself in the never failing childish pleasure of starting a fire. He wasn't particularly skilful at the business but he thoroughly enjoyed it; and eventually after a succession of dubious starts and fresh encouragements the thing began to blaze away merrily.

When eventually most of the stuff had been burnt and Arthur went back into the kitchen to see about getting himself a cup of tea he was astonished to find that the time was already a quarter past five. Half an hour later, washed and tidied up a little and agreeably tired, he sat himself down in the living-room in front of the T.V. set for the evening news bulletin. He was not expecting to hear anything of any particular interest to himself, so that the first words which came out from the screen astonished him. . . .

'. . . *Wymark Mews* . . .'

Arthur sat forward in his chair and stared incredulously at the impassive face of the news announcer blandly making his statement.

'Wymark Mews, a short cul-de-sac close to South Kensington station in London, was the scene this afternoon of a brutal murder. Our reporter Miles Underwood from the spot. . . .'

'About twenty yards from where I am now standing,' Miles Underwood told the world, 'a woman was stabbed to death shortly after three o'clock this afternoon. Mr Frederick Hill, a postman who regularly delivers mail in Wymark Mews, actually saw it happen. Mr Hill, tell me what you saw . . .

Mr Hill, an unassuming little man, obviously shaken by what he had seen, did his best to describe it.

'. . . Well, I had finished my round and cleared up everything and I was walking home going the way I always do which takes me past the top of Wymark Mews. As I went past the opening of the Mews I heard a sort of scream, well, a cry anyway, and I saw a woman come running out of the door of one of the houses. There wasn't time to wonder what was happening before the man came out after her.'

'Was he shouting or calling out?'

'I can't really say. Everything happened in a minute. Less. He caught hold of her, or she turned round to hit him, I'm not sure which it was, anyway there was a sort of struggle and then I saw him hit her—well, I thought he was just hitting her but from what I saw afterwards he must have been stabbing her. The woman fell down onto her knees and then in a sort of heap on the pavement and the man went back into the house.'

'And what did you do then Mr Hill?'

'I went to see if I could help the woman.'

'And were you able to help her?'

'No. Not really. There was a lot of blood coming from her neck and I didn't know what to do about it. Then I remembered there was a G.P.O. telephone box close to the top of the Mews and I ran to it as fast as I could and dialled 999. It looked to me like a police job and I thought I was best out of it.... '

'We understand,' the news announcer continued in his unruffled voice, 'that the woman who has since died in St James's Hospital was Mrs Valerie Peters and that a Mr Jimmy Larning of number five Wymark Mews is now helping the police with their enquiries.

'Accounts are coming in of long queues of cars forming on the roads leading to the Wes—'

Arthur Walker leant forward and cut the man's voice short in mid-word. His hands were shaking and he was white-faced.... *'Christ Almighty,'* he thought, *'what next?'*...

'What next' happened almost immediately. Arthur Walker was a very moderate man in his drinking habits but when he had switched off the news bulletin on T.V. he crossed the room to pour himself out a whisky and soda. He felt that he needed one. He was squirting the soda into the glass when the front door bell rang.

Arthur was mildly surprised. He was not expecting anybody, nor had Molly said that she was. He went into the hall with a vague feeling of apprehension. When he opened the door he found himself confronted by someone whom he instantly recognised....

'Three no trumps,' said Hooky. 'Good afternoon, Major Weller. May I come in?'

Hooky had been an unhappy man ever since his interrupted week-end at Beaconsfield. Feeling sadly in need of solace, moral support and spiritual guidance he had instinctively taken himself to the Moon in search of these comforting things.

Duggie greeted him warmly.

'A very remarkable thing is about to happen, Hefferman,' he said. 'I am offering you a drink. And what is more I have paid Eric here every ha'penny the miserable misbegotten son of an account-cosseting usurer claims that I owe him, haven't I, Eric?'

'Your slate is clean, Mr Findlayson. *Tabula rasa.*'

'God Almighty, dog Latin now from behind the bar; that shows you the state the world is getting into. What will you drink, Hefferman?'

'This evening a brandy, I think.'

Duggie signalled to the barman and said to Hooky, 'You're looking worried.'

'It's a question of conscience—'

'Make that a double, Eric, Mr Hefferman is suffering from an incurable disease. What's her name?'

'Whose name?' Hooky asked.

'The poor deluded innocent female whom you are confusing with what you call your conscience.'

'It's not so simple as that, Duggie—'

Quite genuinely Hooky was not finding his problem all that simple. The more he thought the matter over the more he wished that he could surrender himself wholeheartedly to some vast omnipotent religious Mother who would tell him what to do and whose decision he would accept without qualm.

'Please Father, I feel myself in a moral dilemma.'

'Just tell me the facts, my son, and from what I remember of my days as a theological student at Worcester seminary I'll dig out something from the Summa to meet your case.'

That simple way out wasn't open to Hooky. He had to be his own Summa. It was easy enough to say to himself: a crime has been committed; it involved (although to some extent incidentally perhaps) the life of one woman, and certainly the loss of valuable prop-

erty to another woman, a relative of yours. You know
the identity of at least one person concerned with the
crime; what you must do, therefore, is to go to Hove
C.I.D. and tell them what you know....

It was easy enough to say that, and Hooky heard
himself saying it many times a day. Unfortunately for
peace of mind he also heard himself saying, 'If Janice
Mellard learns that her father is mixed up in this business and if he gets jailed as a result of it, which he
certainly will be, her whole life at home will be blown
to smithereens, to say nothing of what it might do to
her career on the stage....' Strongly though all that
influenced him Hooky was being reluctantly forced to
the conclusion that knowing what he did it was impossible simply to sit back and do nothing. In the end
he came to the somewhat muddled and unsatisfactory
conclusion that he must at least speak to Janice's father. What would come of the meeting he didn't know;
at the back of his mind he had the uncomfortable
feeling that ultimately there would be nothing for it
but to go to the police with such information as he
had, but he was trying to put that off for as long as
possible and going to see Janice's father was a delay-
ing tactic out of which some solution (but he couldn't
think what) might possibly come.

He knew nothing whatever about the Horse Show
at High Wycombe and since, as far as he was aware,
Janice went home only at week-ends he chose Friday
as a suitable day to motor himself down to Beacons-

field. It was a few minutes after six when he stopped the Jag in Rookery Lane and not without trepidation and a feeling that what he was doing would at the best be futile, and might have to turn out to be much worse, rang the bell of Magpie Cottage.

'*Three no trumps. Good afternoon, Major Weller. May I come in?*'

Arthur Walker recognised his visitor instantly, and it never occurred to him that his appearance there at that moment could not be connected with the shattering news given only a few minutes before on the T.V. bulletin. *Christ, this is it* he thought, *it had to come sometime and here it is, now*. He actually glanced over Hooky's shoulder fully expecting to see a police car in Rookery Lane. There was a car there but it wasn't a police car.

'May I come in?' Hooky repeated. 'But before I do, is your daughter here?'

'No. Nobody is but me. I'm alone in the house at the moment thank God, so you'd better come in and get it over.'

Hooky followed through the hall of the cottage and ducking his head a little (he was a tall man and the cottage was an old one) made his way into the living-room. It looked a homely, comfortable, liveable-in sort of place. There were two chintz covered armchairs and a pleasantly shabby sofa. A T.V. set stood in one corner and in another a table with a modest display of bottles and glasses on it. A drink—it looked like a whisky and soda—was standing there already poured out.

'Thank God he's not a teetotaller,' Hooky thought, *'I shall need a drink before this lot is over.'*

He seated himself in one of the armchairs and, unpleasant though it was going to be, decided that he had better get down to business. The neat dapper little man sitting opposite him looked white enough to faint.

'You know who I am, don't you?' Hooky led off.

Arthur Walker nodded. 'Yes, I know you.'

'Ah, but you don't know quite enough, chum. As far as you know I am Mrs Page-Foley's nephew and a pretty chancy caller at Bridge. What you don't know is that I am also a private investigator. Every sort of enquiry undertaken, speed and confidence assured.'

'You're a private investigator?'

'I am. Not the busiest in the world, maybe; but every now and again people employ me. At the moment I am working on a job for your daughter.'

'For my daughter? For Janet?'

'Well, I know her as Janice Mellard.'

'And she knows about Hove?'

Hooky shook his head. 'Not a clue. She hasn't the vaguest idea Major Weller exists.'

'She soon will though, won't she?'

Arthur Walker crossed the room and picked up his glass. He turned suddenly and said, 'Just a minute, though. I don't get this. If Janet doesn't know about Hove what has she put you on to me for?'

'Is that whisky in that glass? And soda?'

Arthur Walker nodded.

'Mix me one will you; I always drink when I'm on duty.'

Walker poured out a generous tot of whisky, splashed some soda into it and handed the glass over.

'Don't go through the farce of drinking my health,' he said, 'not with all this lot we've got on hand.'

'All right, I'll drink to your eternal damnation,' Hooky replied cheerfully, 'because in my book you're a bloody fool.'

'Thanks very much. And do you mind telling me if it isn't the Hove business exactly what it is you are doing for Janet?'

'You've got a damned nice girl in that daughter of yours, Walker.'

'You needn't tell me that. I know it.'

'She's been anxious about you because she says you've been looking worried and upset lately and she thinks you may be going off the rails with some female and it may smash up your home and marriage— any truth in it?'

Walker shook his head.

'No excitable little hot-pants waiting for you in a love-nest somewhere?'

'As it happens I've never looked at any other woman since I've been married to Molly.'

Hooky looked at the little man long and hard. 'It's a funny thing,' he said at last, 'but, do you know, I'm inclined to believe you. You're not in any trouble like blackmail, then, or anything like that?'

'I'm in quite enough trouble thank you. But I'll tell you one thing mister—'

'Hefferman,' Hooky prompted.

'Ah, that's right. Hefferman. I'll tell you one thing, Mr Hefferman, whatever comes out of this I'm sorry about the lady who was with your aunt that afternoon. She never should have been there. We never thought for a moment that anybody else would be there.'

'But she was there,' Hooky pointed out. 'And if there's one thing certain it is that she shouldn't have had such a fright thrown into her that she died a few hours later of a heart attack.'

'God Almighty, no. Probably there isn't much point in my saying this after what happened, but it happens to be true. I was always dead against that sort of thing. I had nothing to do with that. My job—well, you must know by now, obviously, what my job was. The con man stuff. I've nothing to lose or gain now, Mr Hefferman, so I'll just tell the truth. And the truth is, I liked your Aunt. God, one of the old school there all right. And she liked me too. You may not believe that, but she did.'

Hooky took a sip from his glass and looked slowly round the room. The impression it had made on him when he first came in was re-inforced. It looked homely and happy.

'I'd say you had a nice little place here,' he said.

'Don't rub it in. I've everything a man could want.'

'I've known so many crooks,' Hooky said, 'that I realise it's a silly question. But I can't help asking it. When you've got all this, why the other business? What made you start?'

Arthur Walker thought for a moment or two before replying, then he said, 'I could spin you a hard luck story, of course; and incidentally make it sound sad enough for you to cry your eyes out; but it isn't worth it now. It wasn't hard luck, it was my being weak. Plus the fact that there are an awful lot of stupid people in the world. Criminally stupid some of them. I had a good job with a law firm. In time I daresay I would have become managing clerk and done well for myself. But unfortunately for me I found out how silly and trusting some rich old women can be. It's easy to fool people, Mr Hefferman; damn it, you'd think some people want to be fooled the way they go on; and when you find there's money in it—' he made a gesture—'well, there you are. And once you've started—' he shook his head, 'you get caught up in it; it's like a web spinning round you; there are other people to be thought about—or there were,' he added as a grim little afterthought.

I wonder what he means by that Hooky thought studying the little man with the odd mixture of intense interest and half humorous compassion which was his normal outlook on life generally.

'Look, Mr Hefferman,' Arthur Walker continued, 'if you've got a police car coming give them a ring and let it come straight away, before Molly and the daughter get back; will you do that for me?'

'There isn't a police car coming as far as I know.'

'What? Not after what happened in Wymark Mews this afternoon?'

Hooky hadn't heard of Wymark Mews in his life and said so.

Walker stared at him. 'You didn't hear the quarter to six news?'

'I was in the car on my way here.'

Walker silently carried their two glasses over to the corner of the room and recharged them. When he handed Hooky's back to him the little man said, 'Well, there's no point in trying to keep quiet about it because a chap actually saw it happen—a postman going by...'

'Saw what happen?'

'That bloody fool Jimmy Larning and that knife of his; he stabbed her. Ran out of the house after her and stabbed her. Practically in the street. This postman chap saw him do it.'

'Who was it he stabbed?'

'Val. The woman in the team. Well, she *was* the team practically. She thought the whole scheme up in the beginning.'

'These are the two people in the business with you?'

'Of course they are. That's what I'm trying to tell you, or they *were*. Val's dead now, she died in St James's the news said and the Law has got hold of Jimmy. He's helping the police with their enquiries, which means he'll help himself to a fifteen years' stretch for murder I shouldn't wonder.'

Hooky digested this remarkable news in silence for some seconds and it was Arthur Walker who spoke again first.

'I've never been more shaken in my life I can tell you. I put the news on just for something to listen to and, Christ, all this lot came out at me, the chap mouthing away at it as though it was something that had nothing to do with anybody. Just before you came in.'

'I knew absolutely nothing about it,' Hooky assured him.

'No. Well, I suppose you couldn't have done. I see that. But you do know that I was mixed up in the Hove business at your Aunt's flat, so like I said a moment ago let's get it over and done with. There's the telephone. Get the police out here; they can have me and the snuff-boxes just as soon as they like. I wouldn't dream of trying to run away. It's not worth it.'

Hooky made no movement towards the telephone. Eventually he asked,

'Where are the snuff-boxes, then?'

'The snuff-boxes we took from Mrs Page-Foley's flat in Hove are in a blue bag—a sort of air-travelling bag I'd call it—locked up in the bottom drawer of the chest of drawers in my bedroom upstairs, just above us.'

'Go and get them.'

With a few minutes Arthur Walker was back in the living-room carrying a soft-sided dark blue bag which he was about to open.

Hooky stopped him with a gesture.

'Are the Arberton snuff-boxes in there?' he asked.

'Every one of them.'

'Right. Don't bother to open it. I believe you.' Hooky reached out and took possession of the bag. 'I'll see they get back to my Aunt,' he said, 'and that will be the end of that.'

Arthur Walker stared at him in silence for some seconds.

'How do you mean, *that will be the end of that?*' he asked at length.

'Well,' Hooky answered brightly, '—I recognise that it's probably an optimistic statement taken in any wide sense. As far as stealing my Aunt's snuff-boxes is concerned I've got them back; two of the people involved seem to have settled their own hash pretty thoroughly and as for Lady Bitterne's death I accept that you personally had no direct responsibility for it, so I think it's fair to say that that particular episode has tidied itself up pretty neatly. Like I say, that's the end of that. But knowing what bloody fools most crooks are I'm inclined to think that in spite of having a home like this, and a wife and daughter who obviously mean a lot to you—in spite of having all that, my guess is that after you've got over the scare of this you won't be able to resist starting the same sort of thing over again with other partners, somewhere else—'

'You think once bent always bent?'

'For the sake of Janice I'd be delighted if you would prove me wrong,' Hooky said. 'But no man is ever going to catch me preaching sermons, or moralising. If you want to chuck up your happy little private paradise and go marching off to hell, you do it. That's your concern and I think you'll do it.'

He rose, holding the blue bag.

'Obviously you won't tell Janice I've been here,' he said, 'and I shan't say anything about it to her either. In fact I shan't be seeing her again. It will be best all round that way. She doesn't want to concern herself with me. Life's just opening up for that girl. She's got a career in front of her. Probably a career of stardom—if her father isn't selfish and stupid enough to spoil it.'

He went out of the room, pulled the front door of Magpie Cottage to behind him and putting the bag carefully on the back seat of the Jag, reversed in the narrow lane and drove off towards London town.

FIFTEEN

'IS THAT YOU, HOOKY?'

Things had been unexpectedly busy in Gerrard Mews lately and the telephone rang very frequently. This particular call was one which Hooky had been expecting, but not wanting; he knew that it had to be dealt with, but he didn't relish dealing with it.

'Is that you, Hooky?' the high clear voice from Lammington Gardens asked.

'None other.'

'And what have you been doing for exercise these days?'

'Nothing.' He made his voice deliberately flat and unencouraging.

'No walks in Richmond Park?'

'I haven't been walking anywhere.'

'No rowing on the Serpentine?'

'I've been too busy.'

There was a short silence, then Janice said, 'Hooky, there's a party, mostly a theatrical affair, on tonight. It will be rather fun I think. I've been asked to bring a man along. Will you come?'

'No thanks.'

There was a longer silence this time; then, in a slightly changed tone of voice, 'Is anything wrong, Hooky?'

'Wrong? What should be wrong? I'm just not interested that's all, I've other things to do.'

'Am I getting the brush-off, Hooky?'

'I suppose you could say that, yes.'

'Well to hell with you then. You men are all the same. Just as long as it's fun for you it's all right, then somebody else comes along and you can't be seen for dust. *Men—*'

'Don't worry about men, Janice. Most of us, as you quite rightly suggest, are bastards. You just get on with your career, you'll find it will be much more satisfactory.'

Having preached which unwilling sermon he put the telephone back on its rest with a decisive gesture of finality. *Must be getting old and out-of-my-mind,* he told himself, *to cross an attractive girl off my visiting list* . . . and he *had* found Janice attractive, no doubt about that; there was something young and fresh and untouched about her. He had a suspicion that she might be foolish enough to fall in love with him, and Hooky knew far too much about himself and was fundamentally too honest to think that that would work.

'Tip your hat and kiss 'em goodbye before you get into trouble,' had always been his motto where the ladies were concerned; but in this particular instance he was doing it to save the lady from getting into trouble... *hope they put it to my credit in the Eternal Ledger* he thought piously. *God knows there'll be plenty on the debit side* ...

Roly Watkins who had come into the room during the last part of the telephone conversation nodded his approval.

'That's a good bit of advice, Mr H, that is, *don't worry about men*. Oh dear, oh dear, if you could only persuade yourself to do the same about the girls.'

'Henceforth I probably shall. Very likely I shall retire into a monastery.'

'Nunnery more like,' Roly said, 'and you'd get 'em all excommunicated. Reverend Mother and the lot.'

'For the moment however, I am not going further than the South Coast.'

'That Honourable Aunt of yours, Mr H?'

'She has a soft spot in her heart for me, Roly.'

'I didn't know she 'ad a heart, Mr H,' his henchman said. 'Steam engine more likely.'

Hooky had invited himself to Hove for a specific reason; he wished to be on hand when a particular event occurred. When he arrived in Wensdale Court he thought he could detect slight signs of weariness in the old warrior; and goodness knows, he thought, at her age she's got every right to be somewhat weary and disenchanted with things; she's seen too much of everything, he thought, too much greed, pride, folly,

stupidity, lust, envy and malice, too much misman-
agement by man of man's affairs....

'And how is Chief Detective Inspector Lewis doing?' Hooky enquired genially.

'I am quite sure the Chief Inspector is working hard
at all the enquires he has to make.'

'Still taking his boxer out every evening for
walkies?'

'I am not concerned with the personal habits of the
police force; as long as they recover my Arberton
snuff-boxes for me which I am quite sure they will
do—' His Aunt stopped suddenly in mid-sentence and
when she went on again her voice was different, it
sounded tired and old— 'Oh Hooky, to be honest I am
not sure that they will. When this horrible thing happened I told myself that I didn't really care much.
Possessions were only possessions and one shouldn't
let oneself get too much attached to them. Possessed
by them. But it isn't true. Not quite true anyway. Not
for an old woman like me. I *do* mind. I was young in
the old world, before everything changed for ever; and
I find you get attached to things of the old, forgotten,
life. I am sure that you must think me a sentimental
old fool, but—' she made a gesture and let her voice
trail away.

'My dear Aunt,' said Hooky speaking slowly and
meaning every word he uttered, 'I can and do assure
you that the very last thing I should ever accuse you of
being is a sentimental old fool....'

The next morning at breakfast (which in Gerrard
Mews frequently consisted of a couple of aspirin and
a look out of the window) his Aunt had entirely recovered her equilibrium. She was as brisk, alert, com-
petent and demanding as ever, too much so for Hooky
at half past eight in the morning. She was in the middle of explaining to him exactly the correct way to
make coffee—'Which hardly anybody is aware of
these days'—when she was interrupted by the front
door buzzer.

She glanced at the clock and said, 'That must be the
postman, and Mrs Perks isn't here yet. Will you see
what he wants, Hooky?'

Hooky was glad that Ada Perks had not yet come,
he wanted to be the one to greet the postman that
morning. He completed the necessary formalities at
the door and came back into the dining-room.

'A large registered packet for you, Aunt Theresa,'
he announced innocently.

'A registered packet for me? Whatever can that be?'

'A gift from some admirer no doubt.'

'I always find your facetiousness tedious, Hooky,'
his aunt said tartly. 'At breakfast time I find it un-
bearable. Open the package, please.'

'Certainly, Aunt.'

The package contained a blue travelling bag. The
blue travelling bag, when unzipped, was seen to con-
tain a number of small articles each carefully wrapped
in tissue paper. Hooky unwrapped one of them and set

it on the table. With splendidly simulated surprise he exclaimed, 'Good heavens, one of your Arberton snuff-boxes.'

His Aunt stared at the box incredulously. 'What an extraordinary thing,' she said at last. 'Are they all there?'

The bag was emptied, its contents carefully unwrapped one by one and set out in rows. They were all there; all forty-two of them. Aunt Theresa stared at them without speaking for some seconds; Hooky had never seen the formidable old lady so *bouleverse* before; for one anxious moment he feared that he might have overdone things a bit and that she might be going to have a heart attack. But Mrs Page-Foley was immune from heart attacks.

'What an extraordinary thing,' she repeated at length.

'Yes, isn't it?'

'Do you know anything about this, Hooky?' she asked with sudden suspicion.

'I? How should I? You must remember my dear Aunt, that I am only an amateur just as you yourself said.'

'Did I? Sometimes I say things which are not entirely justified by subsequent events.' Then with splendid illogicality the old lady went on, all the accustomed fire and decision returning to her voice, 'I always did say that nice little Major Weller was innocent, didn't I?'

'You did, Aunt Theresa, you did,' Hooky acknowledged and then he added, *sotto voce,* 'and perhaps up to a point he was.'

A DEB RALSTON MYSTERY

DEFICIT ENDING

LEE MARTIN

Ready or not, Ralston is back from maternity leave, haunted by
the look of a young teller who is taken hostage and later killed—
the first in a string of victims.

Deb Ralston is soon hot on the tail of the murderers and heading
straight into deadly danger.

OTHER PEOPLE'S HOUSES

SUSAN ROGERS COOPER

In Prophesy County, Oklahoma, the unlikely event of a
homicide is coupled with the likely event that if one occurs, the
victim is somebody everybody knows....

And everybody knows nice bank teller Lois Bell who, along
with her husband and three kids, dies of accidental carbon
monoxide poisoning. But things just aren't sitting right with chief
deputy Milton Kovak. Why were the victims' backgrounds
completely untraceable? And why was the federal government
butting its nose in the case?

"Milt Kovak tells his story with a voice that's as comforting as a
rocking chair and as salty as a fisherman."

—*Houston Chronicle*

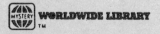

A Sheila Travis Mystery

MURDER

at Markham

First Time In Paperback

PATRICIA HOUCK SPRINKLE

The body of beautiful bad girl Melanie Forbes is found wrapped in an Oriental rug in an unused basement storeroom of Chicago's elite school of diplomacy, the Markham Institute.

Sheila Travis, new administrative assistant to the president, has years of diplomatic experience behind her. Though unfamiliar with the protocol for dealing with a murder in one's new workplace, her nose for crime pulls Sheila—and her eccentric Aunt Mary—into the investigation.

"A delightful new sleuth makes her debut here."

—*Publishers Weekly*

WORLDWIDE LIBRARY
MYSTERY
TM

First Time in Paperback

MIRIAM BORGENICHT

A tragedy turns into a living nightmare when health counselor Linda Stewart's adopted infant daughter is legally reclaimed by the baby's natural teenage mother— and both are found dead two days later.

Linda's agonizing grief is channeled into a burning determination to solve these senseless murders. While suspicions of drug involvement might explain the sudden fortune the young mother had acquired, Linda's subtle probing takes a seedy turn into black-market adoptions.

"Borgenicht's perceptive comments on troubling social issues generate plenty of tension." —Publishers Weekly

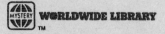